Brutal Prince

Tami Mason

BRUTAL PRINCE

Edited by Rebecca Aksdal

Cover by Shepard Original

Trigger Warnings

This book contains subjects and issues some
may find offensive.

Physical Abuse
Murder
Sexual Abuse
Dubious Consent

For a full list of trigger warnings, please visit
this site: www.TamiMason.com

Prologue

Julia

THIRTEEN YEARS AGO.

The last thing I expected this morning was to be summoned to my father's office. My heart jack-hammered in my chest as I made my way down the imposing hallway. My presence had been requested many times over the years, but each visit ended with me rushing out, in tears. I had no friends. I wasn't allowed to date. My life was lived in a shiny cage made to imply privilege. Whatever he wanted today would be added to the exhaustive list of demands I'd learned to live with.

My palm rested against the cool cherry wood of the door frame while I gathered my courage to lift my fist and knock. The door opened before my fist made contact, revealing my father's personal assistant. He towered over me, and the way he leered made my skin crawl.

I waited until he backed into the room and then gave him a wide berth as I approached my father's desk. My heart continued to beat wildly while I waited for him to speak. He didn't make eye contact, but gestured to a seat across from his desk. "Sit, Julia. I need to discuss something important with you." I slowly sank into the chair. Unable to tear my eyes away, I tracked his movements as he continued tapping out something on his keyboard. His intense gaze never wavered from the screen.

As soon as his eyes shifted in my direction, I swallowed hard, a thousand possibilities running through my head. His stare had my cheeks heating and my heart thumping even harder. The silence between us became deafening. Finally, he condescended to speak. "As you know, the Baldoni family has many traditions to ensure alliances remain strong. We must not show weakness in any form when doing business."

My focus was trained on his face, confused as to why he was telling me this. My father issued orders to others without a moment's hesitation, and his expression told me he was about to issue another command.

I took a sharp breath and steeled myself. He pushed up from his chair and made his way to the arched windows, his eyes falling to something outside. When he turned toward me, a mask of indifference was firmly in place. I held my breath when his brows dipped low before he turned back toward the window. I sat up a little straighter. It was obvious by his hesitation that whatever he needed to say weighed heavily on his mind and chances were it would not make me happy. His eyes met mine through the reflection on the glass. "An opportunity landed in my lap, and it's one I can't pass up."

He continued to study my face, no doubt seeing my confusion. "I don't understand. What does that have to do with me?"

Before I could question him further, he continued. "Make no mistake, Julia. Everything I do is for the good of the family. The leader of a family in Chicago has expanded their business into my territory. Their standing in certain organizations will benefit our family." He ran a hand through his salt and pepper waves. My lips trembled as I tried to process what he was saying. Whatever this business deal was, it had something to do with me.

"Michael Singara is the head of the Singara family. They deal in arms negotiations. We made a deal that secured our authority, not only in Chicago but throughout Michigan, as well as creating some revenue in New York, without the need to deal with the New York boss." He paused before continuing. Something flashed across his face, but as quickly as it appeared, it was gone again. "You and Michael will be married, Julia."

The floor suddenly felt as if it had dropped away, plummeting me into a bottomless pit. My vision blurred, and I struggled to get my bearings. I grasped the chair arms to steady myself and looked at my father like he'd gone mad. "Excuse me. Did you say married?" Surely I'd heard him wrong. I vehemently shook my head. "What if I refuse?"

He narrowed his eyes and tilted his head. "I'm sorry, did I give you the impression you had a choice in the matter? I made a commitment and intend to see it through. The contract has been signed, and you will comply." I opened my mouth, but nothing came out. Was this even legal? Deep down, though, I knew it didn't matter. Laws didn't apply to my family. Anything I could have said would have been pointless. His mind was made up, and there was no changing it.

I stood frozen in place until I felt his hand on my shoulder. Shaking it off, I bolted from the room and ran blindly down the hall toward my bedroom. After I clicked the lock in place, my body slid down the wall as fat tears coursed down my cheeks.

THREE WEEKS HAD passed since my father's solemn declaration had upended my quiet life. I was living in an alternate universe, mindlessly going through the motions each day. I reached out to my mother and, although she sympathized with my situation, she said her hands were tied. I couldn't fathom how she seemed so resigned to her only daughter being sold like this.

I met my future husband. My father and stepmother hosted a black-tie dinner at the mansion the night before, and it took everything in me to hide my feelings when he walked through the door. He wore a black-on-black tuxedo that hugged his broad shoulders and looked as if it were tailored for his body, but I couldn't tear my eyes away from his blond waves and clear blue irises. There was something familiar—had we met before tonight?

His gaze traveled my body before settling on my face. "You must be Julia. It's a pleasure to meet you." He lifted my hand, and the feel of his lips as they brushed my knuckles caused my blood to chill. I stared at this man who appeared the same age as my father. His lips turned up to form a salacious smile.

I opened my mouth, and after a few failed attempts at speaking, I uttered, "Hello, Michael. It's nice to meet you, too." My lips trembled as the lie left my mouth. He released my hand, and with one finger, lifted my chin. His blue eyes turned obsidian as his pupils swallowed his irises, threatening to devour my soul. I shifted nervously, eager to break away. When he cupped my cheek, my eyes closed and I leaned into his palm as was expected of me, despite wanting to pull away from his burning touch.

When the band began to play a slow song, we found ourselves in the middle of the dance floor. I placed one hand in his and slid the other to his shoulder while he wrapped his free arm around my waist and pulled me to him. No words were spoken between us and when the last note died out, he kept his hold tight as he locked eyes with me. Suddenly it all came back. When I was thirteen, I saw this man at the mansion. I can't believe I had forgotten those cold blue eyes.

I blinked away tears as I tried to hold back my emotions. Panic washed over me when he took my hand and led me through the crowd to where my father stood next to several men and women. Excusing himself from his entourage, my father led us down the hall to his office. As soon as the door closed, Michael spoke. "I don't want to wait until she's eighteen to seal this deal. I want to marry her as soon as possible." My gaze shot to my father, who appeared to actually be considering this ludicrous idea. When he finally replied, my heart thundered. "It's settled. The wedding will take place on December eighth."

A gasp flew from my mouth, but knowing it was fruitless to protest, I gave a semblance of a smile and nodded.

I had no control over any aspect of my wedding. Michael's assistant sent briefs detailing everything from food to photos to guest lists. She even had names narrowed down from an approved list to serve as attendants. My father had bridal dresses shipped from Milan and delivered to the mansion, and he insisted I try each before I made a decision. As if I cared which one covered me as I trudged down the aisle to my ill-fated future. As I discarded each lace and satin creation onto the floor, the mountain grew higher and the noose tighter. By the time I slipped off the last one, I was gasping for each breath. Soon I would be forever linked to the Baldoni family, my future set in stone.

When the day finally arrived, it was one more bar added to the shiny cage of my life. Pinpricks erupted over my skin as I took one last glance in the mirror. Moisture gathered in the corners of my eyes, but I vowed not to show any weakness. My fingers clutched the delicate lace of the tapered veil, the soft stitching smooth to the touch. I had chosen a conservative gown made of the softest satin. The sweetheart neckline enhanced my modest bosom and Chantilly lace dripped from the cap sleeves. With every step I took, the hem teased the floor.

The ride to the cathedral was a blur. The limo was packed and voices buzzed all around me, but I heard nothing, lost in a world of my own thoughts. When I entered the cathedral, my footfalls grew louder as they hit the hardwood of the church foyer. My father gave me a terse smile and extended his arm as the stringed quartet hit their first note.

After the attendants walked down the aisle, it was my turn. I managed a counterfeit smile, ensuring it was fixed in place as I slid my arm into my father's and we took our positions. My palms were clammy, and my mouth grew dry. I inhaled a deep breath when my eyes landed on the groom. Clear blue eyes looked into my withering soul.

I swallowed the bile rising in my throat, and my father's hand tightened on my arm. When he ushered me forward, I realized the music had stopped and everyone stood staring at me. I pushed down the throbbing headache and caught my mother's gaze. My eyes pleaded for her to stop this madness, but when she looked away, I knew she was equally helpless.

The music started again and we continued down the long aisle. I recognized the chords of Ave Maria, which might as well have been an ode to death. Each step I took brought me closer to my execution. Not a literal death, but a death to self, to love, to the life I had wanted and dreamed of. Goosebumps dotted my arms and the pulse at the base of my neck thundered out its own chorus. I held my head high and kept my mask firmly in place as we approached the altar. No one would see my emotion, least of all my groom.

I was once again lost in thought when I realized the priest had spoken. Father Vannelli asked who gave the bride away? My father led me forward to complete the tradition—one that was never more true. Except that I wasn't *given* away. I was sold—like cattle. I swallowed hard and continued to look at my father as he all but dragged me to Michael's side and joined our hands.

I lifted my gaze to meet his and forced a smile to hide the quivering of my lips. So much emotion concealed in that one action.

Silence filled the space as the priest continued the wedding ritual. I barely had time to process the words, before Michael gave an enthusiastic "I do."

Father Vannelli turned his attention to me. "Julia Elizabeth Bernard Baldoni, do you take this man…to love, honor and cherish…" My father insisted I use the family name for the ceremony, although I'd never taken it before. It was just a formality. My head snapped up at the word 'obey' and a laugh slipped from my lips before I had time to contain it. This move elicited light whispers from the guests and a scowl from my father. I swallowed my nerves and gave the only allowable response, "I do."

Muffled noises came from someone around me as Michael lifted my trembling hand and slipped the simple gold band onto my finger. "With this ring, I thee wed." His deep rasp vibrated throughout the sanctuary and I turned to my attendant. She smiled and placed his matching band in my upturned palm. I repeated the vow and slid the band over his ring finger.

The stringed quartet began playing softly, bows sliding across the strings of steel, creating the mellifluous melodies of the Canon in D. My eyes slowly lifted to meet Michael's amorous gaze. For a moment I almost forgot I hated him when he took my face in his hands and his lips met mine, leaving me in a terrified daze.

The kiss was only broken by the priest's declaration. "Ladies and gentlemen, I present to you Mr. and Mrs. Michael Lorenzo Singara."

Chapter ONE

Julia

PRESENT DAY.

Lucy is one of my best friends and she's about to get her happily ever after with her handsome fiancé, Jackson. He's one of the formidable King brothers, and my sex-on-a-stick boyfriend, Ben, is another. Jackson and Ben's parents are here. Although their dad looks tired, since he received the news of his cancer's remission he seems more like his old self. Their family and our friends group have spent hours planning this engagement party, from the flowers to the food, and it's perfect for the lovely couple.

As I sit looking out at everyone, I can see the love and support in this room, but somehow, my mind wanders to my past. Growing up as the daughter of a crime boss shaped me into the woman I am today. It taught me to be resilient, no matter what situation I face. Having no friends as I grew up and never being allowed to date, not to mention being forced into an arranged marriage, makes a person desperate for connection, for real relationships—but also autonomy. There's been progress this past year on that last one, as my father suffered a fatal heart attack earlier this year and my half-brother Brando was killed after kidnapping Lucy and me. I wonder what's going to happen next.

It makes sense that my younger brother, Danny, would continue running the daily operations for the family since he's been doing it for the last six months, but it really doesn't matter because I want no part of them or that life. No one in this room—not even Ben, knows my relationship to the Baldonis, and I hope to take the secret of who my family is to my grave.

I'm suddenly brought back to this moment when Lucy approaches our table and gathers me, Tess, and Molly up in a tight hug. We've been best friends since we studied together at Juilliard. Even though Molly is married to Ben's twin brother Courtland and they live in Manhattan, Lucy and Tess are here in Stone Creek, and I go back and forth between the two cities, we've stayed close.

We're seated around the table enjoying a bottle of champagne when the door opens. Jackson's face turns to stone, and he narrows his gaze at the person standing in the doorway. "What the fuck are you doing here, Angie? I don't have anything to say to you." His voice turns lethal, and if looks really could kill, his ex-wife would drop on the spot. She doesn't and everyone's attention turns to the gorgeous dark-haired woman who enters the room.

"That's good. Because I'm not here to talk to you." She turns her gaze toward me, and my face pales. Before anyone can react, she points a finger at me and says, "It's time to face the truth."

Everyone looks at me, while I stare at her, wide eyed, terrified of what she's about to reveal. I'm spared an aneurysm when she continues. "Are you ready to take your place in the family, Sis?" I can't speak or move. I'm trying to process what could have happened to cause her presence here as a firestorm of emotions inflames my already shocked expression. My chest tightens, and I can't seem to catch my breath. When I remain silent, she smirks. "Do you hear me, Julia? You're in charge now."

Relief and confusion battle within me as I stammer and stutter, momentarily forgetting where I am—and who I'm with. "Angie, what the hell are you talking about? After everything that family put me through, why would I want to take over the reins? What about Danny?" Suddenly a curtain of nausea rises in my throat. I attempt to slide my mask back in place, but it's too late. My heart is a drumbeat in my chest when I realize what Angie just announced to the entire room, and what I confirmed. My friends know nothing about my connection with Angie and the Baldoni family. And Ben, my God, what have I done by keeping this truth from the man I love?

"We both know Danny is a loose cannon, and Joey doesn't want any part of it." I ignore her statement and bury my face in my hands. This is a nightmare there's no waking up from. My body heats as I feel all eyes on me.

I didn't ask for this, and I've kept my former life separate from my closest friends and Ben. When I ran away from my husband, I thought I was free from my past. In fact, I haven't seen or heard from that side of the family in over six years, except for my and Lucy's kidnapping six months ago; an event that led to Brando's unfortunate death.

I'm brought out of my pity party by the looks of shock and surprise on my friends' faces. It's excruciating, accelerating my panic and making my chest tighten. My eyes meet Ben's as I lift my head while blinking back tears. His furious gaze pierces me as he speaks. "Julia, what the fuck is she talking about?" I'm consumed by sadness and regret when I see the devastation marking his gorgeous face. I thought my secrets were forever buried, but there are some secrets you can't run from. They always have a way of coming back to bite you in the ass. The walls I've built to protect myself vanish into nothingness as I watch his expression change from disbelief to hurt before finally morphing into barely controlled anger.

My mouth is filled with cotton, and the room is spinning as I try to think of something to say. I never wanted him to know this truth—even if I had, this wouldn't have been how I wanted him to find out. We've been together for almost two years. Why didn't I trust his love enough to come clean about my family months ago? I can tell him about my connection to the Baldonis now and hope to God that he can forgive me, although there's no one to blame but myself if he doesn't. As gutted as I am by the hurt on his face, I know, though, that I can't risk full disclosure. Maybe partial honesty will be enough for now.

Jackson was briefly married to Angie, but that was before I knew him and his family. And I certainly didn't attend the wedding—by that time, I had my own apartment and had left that world behind, or as behind as possible. In my family's line of work, one rarely gets out unless it's in a body bag, but I never considered that the business would fall to me. As long as I can remember, a male always led the family, but I guess that's about to change.

Realizing everyone is staring, waiting for my reply, I release my held breath and offer a weak smile. "Ben, I guess it's time I told you about my family." While we've been dating, I've always made excuses when the subject of meeting my parents came up, at least on my paternal side. I was unprepared to open that Pandora's box and up to now, my stall tactics had served me well.

"I guess you know Angie as your ex-sister-in-law, but to me, she's my little sister." I search his face for some kind of emotion. "I was ten years old when I first met my father. Believe me, it was a shock when I found out who he was all those years ago." Ben's face turns pale, and he stands and begins pacing the room as if he could find understanding in his steps. Finally, he stops and slumps down in the nearest chair. I press my hands against the table and stand. I need to go to him, but he throws up his arm, stopping me in my tracks. A weighty silence fills the room. I fall back into the chair; my chest clenches and salty tears slip down my cheeks.

"You've known who your family is for how long now? Were you ever going to tell me?" Disdain drips like venom, revealing the pain and hurt I've caused. His hands shake, and he can't look at me. The sound of his voice is cold, like he's speaking to a stranger, not someone who shares his bed. I shake my head, needing to explain, but knowing I may have crossed a line to a place there's no coming back from. Would I have told him if my sister hadn't dropped that truth bomb? I know I wouldn't have, but since she did, I owe him some truth.

I want to crawl onto his lap and make him understand. By distancing myself, it was easier to check my feelings. I let down my guard once, and I still bear the scars from doing so. It was safer for my heart to remain closed off. I was sure that falling in love wasn't in the cards for me, and so I didn't expect to fall in love with Ben. It was supposed to be just sex.

Probably sensing a tsunami-sized storm brewing, Angie excuses herself, telling me she'll call later. She chose this face-to-face confrontation, at this particular moment, to make a scene—just like she used to.

I thought I could trust her, that she was different from my brothers, but apparently, that isn't true. Growing up, she had my back even though she was younger. Every time the boys did something and tried to accuse me, she took the blame. We told each other everything. For years she idolized me as her big sister, but as we got older, the distance grew between us.

I watch her until she disappears through the doors. The rest of our friends leave soon after, once I've promised a thorough summary of tonight's revelation. Now Ben and I are alone, and I move to the chair beside him. It's time to tell him the parts that I can, and let the chips fall. My heart breaks, and I need to convince him that what we have is real. Swallowing hard, my gaze locks on his.

"Ben, I'll tell you about my family, and then you can decide if you still want to be with me." His hazel orbs glisten with unshed tears. My heart clenches. I did this to my beautiful man. I'm the one responsible for the look on his face. I had wanted to break away from that life and everything it represented. I had needed someone who hasn't been touched by my family's violence and isn't obsessed with control. And Ben King fit that criteria. When he doesn't respond, I take that as an invitation to continue.

"My mother always told me my father lived far away, but he promised one day to come meet me. When I was ten years old, he made good on that promise. He already had one daughter a little younger than me and three sons, but Brando, the oldest, had it in for me since day one. He was four years older than me, but even so, his jealousy was a constant battle. I walked away years ago with no intention of ever looking back."

Ben's expression turns pensive, and then he stands. Bracing myself for a multitude of questions I'm not ready to answer, I watch him pace the room again, wearing a track across the carpet. When his body comes closer to mine, his eyes darken. I'm still reeling from what could have been when he sits on the table in front of me. He leans forward as I press my body further into the chair.

He cups my cheek, and I realize it's the first time I've felt his touch since Angie's announcement. Guilt consumes me as I close my eyes and lean into his palm. His warmth heats my skin, and my chest heaves as hot emotions skate down my cheeks and my lips quiver. So much tenderness is communicated as his fingers dance across my face. I feel the weight of his gaze on me, and I open my eyes to his devastating smile, the one that could knock a girl up.

He lifts my hand to his mouth, and his lips graze my palm. "Julia, what happened between you and your family?" His beautiful browns urge me to continue.

Pulling away, I take a calming breath and release it. "I lived part time in my father's house until I was seventeen." My chest hitches and he pulls me up and into his lap and rubs circles across my back, soothing the stress away while I rest my head on his broad chest. My head aches from the turmoil of remembering the past.

We stay that way until Ben pulls back and studies my face. "Why did you leave?" My face pales as he waits for an answer. I can't tell him I was sold into an arranged marriage and have been running from my husband for the last twelve years. As much as I want there to be no secrets between us, that boulder-sized one will have to wait. "It's complicated." My eyes plead for him to drop the subject and he must read my mind.

"What time is your flight?"

I hadn't planned to go back to New York until tomorrow, but some problems came up with the music studio I bought last month. Now, with this shit show that just played out, I'm glad I scheduled a flight back for late tonight. Looking at my watch, I answer, "Ten, so I guess I'd better get moving." To be honest, all I really want to do is go to Ben's, crawl under his plush comforter, and hide away from everything, but that won't solve my troubles.

He pulls me back in and holds me close. "I'll take you to the airport."

After several minutes with me tucked safely in his arms, he sighs. His gorgeous browns meet mine and he whispers in my ear. "Julia, baby, you've got this. We'll get through this together."

Chapter TWO

Ben

"What the hell, man? Julia and Angie?" Jackson is usually known for being levelheaded, but this time he doesn't hold back. I'm surrounded by my brothers, who all look at me with the same expression. I asked them to come back to the Lux, the hotel I manage, to rehash the current events. So much shit went down six months ago when Lucy and Julia were kidnapped by Brando, and this new discovery is just the icing on the fucking cake.

Courtland grabs a bottle of Macallan from behind the bar as Knight reaches for glasses. He pours four doubles, and we each down one in one go. I swipe my hand across my mouth while motioning for another. I'm powerless to change the past, but I can damn well get drunk off my ass. I'm hoping this development doesn't change things between Julia and me, but I learned a long time ago never to underestimate fate. She looked so broken, and as much as I wanted to take her pain away, I need distance to process this universe-sized bombshell.

"Look guys, all I know is what you know—Angie showed up tonight spouting bullshit about Julia being next in line to rule the Baldoni family."

A look passes between Courtland and Jackson that I don't like. No one besides Jack was ever supposed to know about my connection with that family—about the accident and Leah's death, least of all my twin, but when Lucy and Julia were kidnapped earlier this year, shit hit the fan, and my brothers were brought on board. This resulted in Brando's death, but that was almost too good for him. Whenever I think about what happened and how it could have turned out differently, I want to kill him all over again. Except this time, I'd choose a slower death. Especially now that I know he was Julia's brother.

I can still see the sheer terror in Julia's eyes when Angie appeared to make her grand announcement. I had long sensed something was off with Julia's family, but never would I have suspected she had ties with one of the most cut-throat crime families since the Capone era. We've been together for almost two years. Her reluctance to disclose her past and why she left her family makes my hackles rise. I don't know how much longer I can let it go.

Maybe if I had been upfront about my connection to the Baldonis, Julia would have opened up. Closing my eyes, my memory of her subtle fragrance of vanilla and jasmine floods my senses as if she were sitting in the room with us. I sit and nurse another drink as my brothers talk among themselves, occasionally addressing me. I nod mindlessly, lost in thoughts of my beautiful girl.

"So, what do you think, Ben?" I'm brought back from my thoughts by Jackson's voice and see everyone looking at me.

"He said, what the fuck are you going to do?" I have no clue what I am going to do. Obviously, I want to come clean about my involvement in that accident years ago—the accident that set everything in motion and sentenced my brother to a lifetime of servitude to Julia's family. But that story isn't solely mine to tell. Jackson has as much to lose as I do. Now that the top two men in the Baldoni family are dead, one of which I was responsible for, could his deal with the devil have died with them?

"Look guys, what am I supposed to do? Julia deserves to know about my past, but it affects more than just me." I slide my gaze toward Jackson as Courtland cuts me off.

"That's all well and good, but don't you think Julia owes you an explanation for this shit show of a family reunion?" He practically snarls. I love my twin, but he's always been rough around the edges and is ruthless to a fault in his business and personal life. Thank God his wife Molly's good nature has rubbed off on him to some degree—but he can still be a heartless dick, especially how he's ridiculing Julia.

I glare at him and never break eye contact. "This isn't her fault. You don't know the entire story." Hell, I don't even know her full story, and I'm trying to give her time, but knowing she's hiding her past from me is a heavy blow. I know she's still hiding something. I should wait until she's ready to tell me, but I'm not sure I can let it go. I really can't judge since I have secrets of my own. My nostrils flare, and I'm seconds away from punching his ass when I feel myself being dragged away and pushed down onto a nearby barstool. I will protect her from anyone, even if it's one of my brothers.

Knight, ever the peacekeeper, has wedged himself between the two of us. Because he's a musician, we tease him that he likes to keep harmony in the family. "Hey, easy, man. Everyone's on edge right now. Let's take a minute to calm the fuck down, okay?"

"Knight's right, Ben. Punching Courtland is only going to bloody your knuckles, and whatever relief you may feel will only be temporary." Jackson's not wrong. Emotions are running high and before I go off half-cocked on my brother, I need to calm down and have another conversation with Julia.

No more secrets. I need to find out if her brothers are going to be a problem, assuming she'll even know. According to her, she hasn't had contact with any of them in years, and I believe her. Whatever happened in her past that made her distance herself had to be devastating, although belonging to a mob family isn't on anyone's wish list. From my own experiences, I have no trouble keeping secrets safe, even to the detriment of my family. I intend to find out every naked detail regarding her family and whatever skeletons are lurking behind closed doors. I just hope she trusts me to protect those secrets.

Chapter THREE

Julia

NINETEEN YEARS AGO.

I was excited about this weekend. I'd been visiting my dad for three years, and this was the first time I got to attend one of the fancy parties he and my stepmom, Maria, threw at the mansion. Maria had taken me shopping with my younger sister, Angie, for the perfect dress for tonight. The one we'd chosen was crimson red with white flowers dotting the Peter Pan collar. The full skirt hit just below my knees, and the way it swirled around my body when I twirled made me feel like a princess in a fairy tale.

When I got downstairs, I saw that a long table had been placed along one side of the room. It was reserved for the children of my father's business associates. The girls got to attend these parties as soon as they turned thirteen, and since I had just celebrated that birthday a week ago, I was invited into the inner sanctum. At least that's what my mother called it when I told her about the party. The boys got to come at age twelve—that's why my twin brothers were here. Angie won't be attending for another two years. I took a glass of sparkling grape juice from a waiter and walked over to find my seat.

My older half-brother, Brando, stood against the back wall talking to his girlfriend, and my other two brothers were lingering around the food tables talking to a couple of boys who looked to be my age. I'm not sure what I did to piss him off, but every time I made eye contact with Brando, his glare said I'd better watch my back. I had tried to be his friend when I first came into the family, but he told me in no uncertain terms that he didn't need a bastard sister, and I had better not get in his way.

The rest of the night passed with little fanfare. My father stood most of the night talking to a man with the bluest eyes I had ever seen. I don't usually pay attention to those kinds of things, but the way they reflected the lights in the room was captivating. I spent the time with a couple of girls my age I had met right after I started visiting my father. We'd hung out a few times, although it was always on my turf and under the watchful eyes of Maria and her entourage of bodyguards. I swear, I'd never seen as many suited men as I had in the past three years. There was something about their larger-than-life presence that made me pause.

When the guests began to leave, I said goodnight and padded to my room. I slipped on my gown and slid into bed, closing my eyes and shutting out the world.

I felt like I had just fallen asleep when sunlight streamed through the bedroom window and my eyes fluttered open. Pink and purple brush strokes painted the early morning sky.

After Brando's death glare last night, I decided to close myself in my room until everyone had left for the day. When I finally walked toward the dining room, I heard music coming from the hallway that led to the gym. Curiosity got the best of me, and I was drawn to the shadows coming from the room.

Stopping short, my hand went to the gym door, the glass cool against my warm palm. My eyes widened when I peeked inside. One man lifted weights to the beat of the music, while another was on his phone. I stood mesmerized as the second man reached into his gym bag and pulled out a gun and turned my way. Swallowing what felt like a boulder, I spun around and took off toward my room determined to lock myself away again, hoping he hadn't seen me.

Leaning against the closed door, my chest heaved as I struggled to breathe. Footsteps stopped outside my door. Holding my breath, I listened as a man's voice said something and another man's voice responded. After what felt like forever, they continued, their steps getting lighter the further away they walked. Only then did I release my breath and sink to the floor. I sat with my knees pulled up and my arms wrapped tightly around them as hot tears streamed down my cheeks. It was the first time I'd seen a gun, and my naivety about my father's world vanished.

Chapter
FOUR

Julia

I t's still dark outside when my eyes flutter open. The last several hours had my mind in a tailspin, triggering memories I'd long let go. Or at least, I thought I had. Now it seems those memories have returned to haunt my dreams.

The rain is making a tapping sound as it hits my bedroom window. I made it back to Manhattan at roughly one o'clock, and now I'm waking up alone instead of in Ben's arms. Closing my eyes, I long for his masculine scent of sandalwood and spice to invade my nostrils. I could stay like that forever, wrapped in a safe cocoon of testosterone and muscle. But, as much as I want to hide, my two worlds collided last night like a fiery meteor crashing into Earth. Before I said goodbye to him at the airport, he said I had this, that together we would be alright. Together seems like an impossible word, especially since I'm still hiding a big part of my past.

I flip on the coffeemaker and sink onto the vinyl bar stool as I focus on the steam rising from the ancient machine. I swear, every time I use it I expect it to give up the ghost. While I wait for my coffee,

I scroll through social media and see Ben's text as soon as it comes through.

> Ben: Morning, Sunshine. Just checking to see how you're doing.

Smiling to myself, my heart leaps and I quickly tap a reply.

> Me: Hey, you. I'm hanging in there. How are you?

I hold my breath as bubbles dance across the screen, stopping and starting again before a text comes through. Except for a quick text letting him know I made it home, we haven't talked since he left me at the airport last night. He'd said he was going to talk to his brothers; I don't know what to expect after *that* meeting. I don't have to wait long for his reply to come across the screen.

> Ben: I'm good. I'm thinking about coming up in a few days. We still have a lot to talk about, don't you agree?

Frowning, I tap out a response.

> Me: You're not wrong. Yes, this weekend would be perfect. Hey, I need to get ready for work. Can we talk later tonight?

> Ben: Sure. Later, Sunshine.

As I smile and toss my phone back on the counter, it immediately begins to ring. Picking it up, I notice it's an unknown number. My heart immediately takes a nosedive, and pinpricks erupt across my flesh. I don't normally answer calls that I don't recognize, but after last night's confrontation, and against my better judgment, I tap the accept button.

"Hello." My voice is shaky, and my mouth goes dry when a familiar, cold voice comes across the other end.

"Well, well, big sister. Looks like Angie talked some sense into you and you're finally ready to take your place in the family." My blood runs cold as Danny's slimy voice fills the silence.

"What do you want, Danny?" My tone is biting. I don't have time for his bullshit. I'm not afraid anymore. Growing up, they'd never missed an opportunity to blame me for their less than stellar activities. I remember being punished for defacing our father's heirloom desk when Brando was the one who carved that obscenity into the antique mahogany. Any time we were not supervised, they would lure me to the attic and lock me in for hours at a time. After I got married, he and Joey didn't have their target at their fingertips. Once I left, I'm not sure how they occupied their time, but I know for damn sure it wasn't by bullying me.

"Easy Sis. What's got your panties in a twist? Or should I ask, who's got them all tied up?" I huff an indignation before he continues, his voice sharper than before. "Tell me about Ben King."

I feel the blood drain from my face. "Why are you involving Ben?" I try to stay calm, but the grasp on my phone is so tight, I wouldn't be surprised if it cracked beneath my grip. "Have you been keeping tabs on me?"

"Do you really think we didn't know what you've been up to since you bailed on your marriage? Remember when he showed up and shot Brando to save you?" I wince when the memory plays in my mind. "We know everything about you, Julia Bear." I cringe at his use of that nickname. He and Joey came up with that endearment shortly after our first encounter, and by that, I mean after the first time they locked me in the attic because I laughed behind Brando's back about some ridiculous joke he'd told. They'd been willing to do anything to be in his good graces.

Squaring my shoulders as if he can see the gesture, I raise my voice and hold nothing back. I'm not that teenage girl anymore.

"Why are you calling me, Danny? You know my position when it comes to the family." I haven't decided what I'm going to do now.

Apparently, I'm next in line to rule this disgusting empire, but I can't tell him that.

I guess I really don't have much choice in the matter as running from tradition could cause a turf war. I need to find out where their soldier's loyalties lie and take it from there. If they land squarely on my side, then I am confident in my control.

"As next in line, should something unfortunate happen to you, I need to be kept in the loop. Joey and Angie both agree we need to meet and settle some things before any more time passes. What would happen if Loverboy found out you aren't the pristine little angel he thinks you are? Stay close. I'll be in touch." With that, the call disconnects. *What the actual fuck? Is he threatening my life? Or worse, is he threatening to tell Ben about Michael?* White, hot anger burns across my cheeks. Before I can think better of it, I'm hurling the phone across the room, flinching when it bounces off the hardwood, shattering into a dozen pieces. Ugh. That's what I get for being hot-headed.

Wrapping my arms around myself, I slide to the floor, unable to catch my breath as what he said taunts me. *What would Loverboy say if he found out you aren't the pristine little angel he thinks you are?* After years of enduring my brothers' bullying tactics, I thought I had put the past behind me, not expecting it to rear its ugly head after all this time. I should have known this would come back to haunt me.

Pushing myself up, I barely have time to make it to the sink before bitter bile makes its way up, splashing the porcelain basin in front of me. A few moments pass before I have control over the somersaults invading my stomach. I turn on the water and wash away the evidence of my unfortunate puke fest.

I'm still wearing my sleep shorts and tank top two hours later as I curl up on my couch, whiskey in one hand and my laptop balanced precariously on my lap. I rarely drink anything stronger than a glass of wine unless I'm on edge, and with everything that's happened in the last twenty-four hours one could surmise that I'm on the fucking edge. In fact, I may have toppled over said edge.

I open my laptop and log in. Notifications are piled one on top of the other—I don't have it in me to deal with them now and swipe to delete them all. I check in with the music studio to make sure things are in order. The assistant I hired when I acquired the studio had sent several emails regarding increased enrollment numbers that will require the addition of three new classes after fall recitals. Now instead of my program being centered solely on piano, we'll be starting violin and vocal lessons, as well. At least staying busy will be a good distraction from the chaos around me. I'm staring at the computer screen when a familiar ring alerts me to an incoming video call. I see it's Molly, and my lips curve upward.

"Hey Molly." I'm looking at my friend, who isn't showing the same enthusiasm about seeing me on her screen.

"Jesus, Julia, why aren't you answering your phone? Ben is freaking the fuck out, and Courtland is about to bust down your door. What's going on?"

"My phone broke. I'm sorry I caused everyone to worry." Oops—no wonder there were so many notifications. I try to come off as casual, but my voice cracks as my friend continues to glare at me through the screen.

"Uh-uh, try again. Jules, what the hell's going on?" Taking a deep breath, I steel myself to have this conversation. She listens as I recount my past, beginning with the acknowledgment that Carmine Baldoni, ruthless crime boss and feared businessman, was, in fact, my father. My vision becomes blurry and I swallow a giant lump; it's difficult to get the words past my tight throat. "There's more, Molly. Something no one besides my family and their close friends knows." The words burn the tip of my tongue. A wave of soul-deep sadness washes over me before I find the strength to continue. "When I was seventeen, my father sold me to another man. We were married and I lived with him for three years."

The shock on my friend's face is palpable and I immediately want to take the words back. But it's too late. "Julia, my God. You're married? I don't understand." I don't miss the tremble she tries to hide as she speaks.

"I'm sorry I didn't tell you, and I know I have no right to ask, but I need you to keep this secret."

"Jules, Ben doesn't know about your marriage?" Although the question is asked, there's no judgment in her tone. I silently shake my head, afraid to open my mouth. I force a weak smile. "I want to tell him. But I need time. Please give me that. I'm sorry for asking you to keep this from Courtland, but I'm not ready yet."

I manage to hold my tears at bay until I look her in the eye and see a stream of salty rivulets skating down her cheeks. The hurt that one of my best friends is feeling is so monumental I glance away before I lose it—or maybe it's something else and I'm totally misreading the situation. Something akin to anger flashes in her blue eyes before she tamps it down and clears her throat before speaking again.

"Jules, I just wish you had trusted me enough to tell me this. I mean, God, we've been friends for years. To say I'm shocked would be the understatement of the year. Even when Ben killed Brando, you never mentioned your connection. Why not?" I wince at his name, but she's right. I should have trusted her, of all people. We told each other everything, and Ben, my perfect Ben, how can he ever forgive me?

"Oh Molly, the only answer I can give you is that I was afraid. Everything happened in a vacuum—and long before I met Ben. I hated my father for what he did, and I was married to a man who abused me every day until I wanted to disappear. My mother helped me break away as soon as she learned the truth." Just then, another call comes through. I'm not surprised when I see his name flash across the laptop screen.

"Hey, Molly, Ben's calling. Can I call you later after I replace my phone?" I still can't believe I was impulsive enough to lose control like that.

"Of course. Later. Love you, Jules."

"Love you, too, Mol."

I quickly switched over to connect with Ben. My heart is thumping wildly when his face appears in all its tantalizing glory.

I try to hide the tremble in my voice. "Hey." I can tell by the way his brow furrows, he's terrified. Molly told me as much, so I decide to take control of the conversation. "I broke my phone. I'm sorry I didn't reach out sooner."

I barely get the words out before he sighs. "My God, Sunshine. Do you have any idea what's been running through my mind? Wait." His concerned expression turns murderous. "What the fuck happened?" He must see my tear-stained cheeks and raccoon eyes.

"Ben, I'm okay, nothing happened. I was just talking to Molly and, you know, emotions and all." I hope that is enough to shut his questions down. In case it's not, I try to change the subject.

"Where are you?" It's the first time I have taken in his surroundings, which look very much like the Charleston airport. "Are you taking a trip?"

"Damn right. I'm on my way to Manhattan."

"Ben. I'm fine. I don't need you to come to New York now," I whisper.

"No way, Sunshine. If you're crying, you need me." He drags his hand through his chestnut waves and his expression softens. "Baby, my plane lands at six. I'll Uber to your place if that's okay."

"No. I mean yes. I mean no, I can pick you up." He chuckles at my indecision and that laugh makes butterflies erupt in my belly. "God, I need you." A fire lights my soul. I didn't know how much I needed him until he uttered those words. I take a sharp breath and a smile tugs at my lips.

His expression turns salacious, and his mouth twitches. Tingles spread across my flesh as he lowers his eyes. "Julia, you have no idea the things I'm going to do to you tonight." He growls as he wiggles his eyebrows. "Your punishment for causing me worry will just be an appetizer. Get some rest, Sunshine, because you're going to need it."

The screen goes black, and I blink nervously at the blank space for several beats. I'm equally turned on and filled with apprehension as I contemplate the events to come.

Chapter
FIVE

Julia

NINETEEN YEARS AGO.

Brando must have been lurking in the hallway and watching as I slipped away from the gym door this morning. Now he's lured me to the attic—again, to torment me. "You little whore!" Malice dripped from his mouth. I shook my head. When he grabbed my arm, I tried to get away, but his hold tightened, and he continued spewing hatred. "Are you trying to fuck up the deal? Do you think he will look at you the same way again? Want to touch you?" What deal? Who is he talking about? He released me with a shove, and I was flung across the cold, plank floor, landing on my hands and knees.

He strode from the room. When I heard the lock click in place, I jerked out of my stupor and banged relentlessly against the wooden door. After what felt like a lifetime, but was likely only minutes, the door opened, and this time, my two younger brothers blocked the doorway.

My relief quickly turned to panic when they entered and Joey closed the door behind them. He leaned against it, arms folded across his chest. "What are you doing? Let me out." I tried to walk past them, but Danny grabbed my hair and shoved me to the floor. "That's for almost ruining the deal. It's Brando's job to make sure you don't fuck it up. You could've gotten him in trouble." My brothers liked to scare me with their words, but they'd never been physical before. I was more than a little afraid that that was about to change as Joey sauntered over to where I cowered.

"Hold her, Danny."

Danny reached down and pulled me up. I tried to break free from his grasp, but he spun me and grabbed my shoulders from behind, pinning my arms behind me.

Despite its tremble, I held my chin high and tried to maintain my resolve. His grip grew tighter and the stretch was almost too much. I watched as Joey reached into the closet and pulled a metal coat hanger from the rod. When he walked toward me, Danny tightened his hold even more, and I became paralyzed by fear. Joey stopped in front of me. My eyes widened and I shook my head. "What are you doing?" My words came out in broken breaths. Anticipating the pain, I closed my eyes and waited to be struck. After a few terrified seconds, I opened them in time to see Joey's arm fly back and bring the cold metal against my side. "Argh." I screamed out in agony. Danny's hands were the only things that kept me upright. Tears burned my throat as I held Joey's gaze. I tried to form words, but none would come. Squeezing my eyes shut, I felt the hard metal come down again and again until Danny released my arms and I sank to the floor trying to find my breath.

I was lying there, eyes closed, when I heard the door open once again. My eyes fluttered and just before they disappeared, Joey spoke. "If you have any thoughts about telling Daddy about this, don't or you'll find out just how bad it can get." With that, they left the room, their taunting laughter following them down the stairs.

Fire coursed through my insides, but I somehow dragged myself down the stairs and into my room without being seen. Closing the door, I fell against it and tried to ignore the stabbing pain that radiated throughout my side. I replayed the last hour in my mind and wondered how I had landed in this hell, and if I would ever escape the flames. Little did I know, this was only the beginning.

Chapter SIX

Julia

I'm startled from whatever this is—a dream or a memory, as I lay here folded in Ben's strong arms, the feel of cool satin brushing softly against my skin. This is where I feel safest, tucked away from my past and the demons that lurk there. His shallow breathing lets me know he's still asleep. After his call yesterday, I picked up a new phone before heading to the airport. When we got back to my apartment, we were exhausted from the events of the last twenty-four hours. We fell asleep with me cradled in his arms.

I carefully slip out of bed and head to the kitchen for my usual morning dose of caffeine.

I'm sitting at the bar drinking coffee when movement catches my eye. Turning my head, my breath quickens as I take in his beauty—his lean, sculpted body and the way his biceps flex as his arms bracket the doorway. My magnificent god. He's deliciously sinful in a pair of low-hanging joggers and no shirt. His irresistible abs make my heartbeat skip and my mouth water. His chestnut hair is tousled from sleep, making him especially sexy. A light smattering of brown hair dusts his chest, and I glimpse the tattoo that runs down his bicep. The one I've become obsessed with. The stark contrast of the black and white dragon with a flower on its tail, and the wicked way the ink crawls down his arm, provides the perfect canvas for my fingers to trace. He smiles, and whatever brain cells I have left suddenly leave the building, but when he speaks, it's his gravelly voice that does me in.

"Morning, Sunshine. You left." I press my thighs together to relieve the pressure building and unconsciously bite my bottom lip.

Moving away from the doorway with the grace of a panther, Ben leans down and places a chaste kiss on my forehead as he tucks a wayward strand of hair behind my ear.

I'm pulled out of my lust-filled stupor when he steps back, moves a stool right next to mine, and takes a seat next to me. It's only then I'm able to form a coherent phrase. Biting my bottom lip and sucking in a deep breath, I answer.

"I'm sorry. You just looked so peaceful that I didn't want to wake you. After the last couple of days, the thought of an uninterrupted night's sleep was too good to ruin. I see you found me, though."

"Jules, we need to finish the conversation we started before you left Stone Creek. I know you need time to process everything, and I do, too. For better or worse, we need to figure out how to navigate this new normal as a team." I lift my gaze to meet his, and tamp down the all-consuming guilt that riddles my soul. He isn't wrong. I've carried my past alone long enough. When we first started this, it was just fun, no strings attached. As soon as I realized it was turning into more than just sex, I should have trusted what we had. We've been a couple for almost two years and it's time I allow him to shoulder my burdens with me—to be my partner in every sense of the word. But so much time has passed and I'm terrified of losing him if he learns the entire truth now. Releasing a breath, my eyes find his, and tingles spread across my sensitive flesh as he brushes his fingers lightly up my arm.

Clearing my throat and leaning away from him, I speak, low and weak, like I'm talking to myself instead of the man beside me. Anxiety bubbles in the pit of my stomach as I decide how much truth I trust myself to tell. "Danny called me yesterday." Something flickers in his eyes as he studies my face before pulling me back into his arms and rubbing circles across my back. I relay the conversation back to him, telling him about the overt threat. At least I can share that much.

"I'll kill him." He pulls back, holding me at arm's length. His eyes have gone completely black, and I know he wants to say more, but he's holding back, and I won't push him, not yet. Instead, I do what distracts us both from the cares of the world, though it's a temporary diversion. I move to straddle his lap, allowing his thick erection to settle between my legs, while strangled moans escape his mouth. I shamelessly grind my desire onto his, over and over until he grabs my chin forcefully and, leaning in, growls in my ear. "Be careful what you ask for, Sunshine. Fire is hard to control once the flames are fanned."

Suddenly, I'm no longer in charge. I find myself flipped around and bent over the bar, his erection hot and hard against my backside. I'm panting as he lowers his mouth to my ear and utters my favorite words in his sexy rasp. "You are mine, Julia." He feathers kisses down my shoulder. Chills ghost along my arms as he slips a hand under the thin silk of my camisole. A rush of air escapes my mouth when his fingers find my nipples and squeeze lightly as they pebble into stiff peaks. The sensation is not enough. I need more. A moan bursts from my mouth. Rolling my head back, I press my thighs together in a feeble attempt to relieve the building pressure between my legs.

Our ragged breaths are in sync as he slides my shorts down my thighs and then off, before nudging my legs apart. His fingers continue their pleasure-filled assault on my nipples while his other hand pushes at my upper back, the granite cool through my camisole, his thin joggers the only thing separating us from heaven. He gives a couple of playful thrusts as I turn to face him. I'm reaching for the waistband of his pants when a shrill sound resonates inches from where I'm pinned to the bar. Groaning, our eyes shoot daggers at the screen. Still reeling in a lust-fueled haze, I slide under Ben's arm while he snatches the phone from its resting place with enough force that it's a miracle it remains intact.

Reaching for my shorts, I shimmy into them and settle on a stool as Ben leans across the bar, agitation etching his gorgeous face. His brothers have impeccable timing, but I guess when you run a hotel, you're expected to be available at a moment's notice. Knight manages the Lux anytime Ben leaves town, and if he's calling this early, it must be important.

"Knight, what do you want?" His voice holds irritation. I suck in a sharp breath and, for a fleeting moment, I feel sorry for his younger brother. I pick up my coffee and continue to stare at him across the upturned mug. I can't hear what Knight says back. "I'm sorry, man." He purses his lips. How can anyone have such a sensuous mouth? It should be a sin. When his eyes meet mine, his expression is apologetic, and I simply nod in agreement.

"Look, man, don't worry." I slide off the stool, my hand reaching for the hem of my camisole and slowly, seductively, I pull it over my head, letting it drop to the floor. I turn and take a step, then look back over my shoulder and give a slow blink as I continue toward the bedroom. He licks his lips, and his eyes are hooded as a sinful smirk plays across his mouth. "Yeah, I'll get there as soon as I can." My footfalls get faster as he ends the call and prowls toward me. "Oh Sunshine, not so fast. We need to finish what we started." And the chase is on…

Chapter
SEVEN

Ben

After I end the call with Knight and engage in a little *morning delight* with Julia, we make plans to return to Stone Creek. Julia makes arrangements with her manager to cancel her classes for the week to come back to South Carolina with me. My brother, the budding rock star, has been called to fill-in for a classical rock band in a neighboring state, but at least he had the forethought to arrange a car to pick us up from the airport. Since I was out of my mind with worry when I couldn't reach Julia, I had asked him to drive me to the airport instead of taking my car.

It's after five when we arrive at the Lux. I hand a key card to Julia for the suite I use here and head to the bar. Checking in with the staff, I answer a few emails before grabbing a bottle of Bordeaux and heading to the room.

When I open the door, my eyes widen, a spark of heat rises in my chest and my blood rushes south. *Fuck me.* There, in front of me, sits the woman of my dreams—the one who holds my heart and soul in the palm of her hand. This strong woman has spent the better part of her life hiding from herself, held mentally captive by the family that should have protected her.

She's changed out of her travel clothes into a silk kimono with a sash tie. She's reclining on a chaise and the kimono is gaping open, showing off the indent of her flat stomach and the slight swell of her breasts. Her eyes are closed and she's sleeping, so I take a moment to appreciate her ethereal beauty. Her dark hair is fanned out over her shoulders, falling seductively onto her perfect breasts. She looks untouched, but also like a Greek goddess. Aphrodite, the goddess of love, lust, beauty, and an array of other qualities that are essentially Julia Bernard. The silk hugs the curve of her hip and begs to be caressed. I know she is exhausted, so I let her sleep.

After placing the wine in a chilling bucket, I settle on the loveseat and open my laptop. Since I'm only a few steps from the office, there's no need for me to stay in plain sight. Whatever issues come up can be resolved from here. Bringing up the surveillance cameras that show the main ballroom and bar areas, I scan the images for anything out of the ordinary.

I'm still not sure if Danny or Joey are planning retaliation for Brando's death, but according to Julia, Danny and Angie think they need to meet and discuss the future. *The fuck she will.* Not unless I'm by her side.

Sensing movement out of the corner of my eye, I feel soft hands land on my shoulders. I set my laptop aside and twist around, then pull Julia into my arms for a playful kiss. She laughs, causing my cock to jerk. God, what this woman does to me. She settles on my lap, and I fear by the way she's moving, coupled with her sexy giggles, that I might not survive tonight.

"Sunshine, you're awake."

"Um-hum," is all she gets out before I capture her lips in another kiss, this one a mix of desire and need—the desire coursing through my veins and my need to own her, mind, body, and soul completely and unashamedly.

Breaking away, I reach for a strand of hair that has fallen across her cheek and tuck it behind her ear. Letting my fingers linger on the nape of her neck, I'm lost in her honey-brown eyes, illuminated only by the small lamp in the corner of the room.

I'm staring at those dark orbs as she tilts her head and wiggles away from my embrace. Taking my hand she pulls me toward the king bed that's adorned with an array of pillows and then she allows the silk to fall away from her perfect body.

"Damn, Jules, so perfect." She stands in front of me, and I can't help myself as I rake my gaze over her body, taking in the delicate curves of her hips and how her nipples stiffen against the cool air. Bending down, I brush my lips lightly over each one, and her body trembles as I tug one into my mouth and gently suck. The way her body writhes ignites my primal need to own her. She's the only woman who has ever consumed me like this. She is the sun, moon, and stars, and I intend to show her just how much she means to me.

There's an awakening taking place inside me. When she arches toward me, pulling at my clothes and scrambling to grip the hem of my shirt, shoving it over my head, I lean forward, my bare skin connecting with hers. I feel her body shudder when she throws her head back in wild abandon.

"Please, Ben. I need you." She reaches for the button of my pants, her desperation quickening my movements, and what I intend to be slow, simmering lovemaking suddenly morphs into fast, hard, soul-stopping carnal need.

My mouth covers hers in a hungry kiss, until I break away long enough to ask, "What do you need?"

"Everything." Her request saturates the air and just looking into her sexy eyes has me ready to spill my load, and I'm not even inside her. She reaches again for the button on my slacks, and this time I don't stop her, and we work together to slide my pants and boxers to the floor.

Her breaths come fast and shallow as I push her onto the bed. I settle my weight on her and run the head of my cock through her soaking core before lining it up at her entrance and slowly pushing inside her. She's always tight, so I only push in an inch or two before pulling out and driving back in a little at a time until I'm fully sheathed in her sweet heat. I give her a moment to adjust before my thrusts begin. When her eyes close and she lets out a low hum, I can't help the growl that comes out of my mouth.

"Open your eyes, Sunshine. I want you to watch as your pussy devours my cock. I want to see the look in your eyes when you shatter around me." On command, her eyes pop open, and her blown pupils convey exactly what I want them to. She's lost in a lust-fueled haze. Our grunts and moans increase in volume and intensity as I move inside her, and she meets every thrust. Feeling my climax barreling down, I want to make sure I take care of her. Slipping a hand between us, my fingers find what they're searching for, stroking that tight bud. My thumb increases the pressure as it circles the tiny nerves until she's crying out her pleasure while I continue to drive faster and deeper, seeking my own release. As I come with a guttural cry, our eyes never drift from each other, and I'm lost in an amber sunset.

I remain buried in her sweet pussy for a few minutes while we both come down from our highs. Rolling off her, I slide over and pull her into my arms; she rests her head against my chest as I trace tiny patterns across her back with my fingers. After a few quiet moments, her body relaxes and her eyes close, and for the first time since this shit show began, I believe we can get through this together. I want to help her, but it's hard when it feels like she's still holding a part of herself back. I don't know how to get her to open up completely and it's killing me. It's glaringly obvious she's afraid of something—or someone. At least for her sake and mine, I hope I'm wrong.

Chapter
EIGHT

Julia

Coming back to Stone Creek was the right thing to do. Even if *my* personal life is going to shit, I can still celebrate with my friends. After our sexcapades last night, I feel somewhat better about my and Ben's situation. Our loving didn't change my circumstances, but it did provide a temporary escape from my cruel reality. Ben hasn't abandoned me, and he proved that by coming to New York. I didn't realize how much I needed him. But could I really blame him if he did abandon me? It was my choice to keep that part of my life hidden from everyone I cared about. So, the fact that he didn't run screaming is a relief. What would he say if I bared my entire soul? I hope I never find out. I have no intention of telling him about my marriage if I can avoid it, but I also know the truth has a way of coming out when we least expect it. For now, waking up with his warm arms wrapped around me feels like a gift I'll treasure for as long as it lasts.

After sliding out of bed, I press my lips to the side of his head in a quiet kiss. I dress quickly then make my way to the lobby and into the bistro. The waiter brings my favorite cup of Stone Creek Espresso.

They must have this java patented because in all the years I've visited, I've never been able to find or replicate this brew.

I'm sipping a decadent cup of heaven when my phone buzzes. Picking it up and seeing my mother's name flashing across the screen fills me with a mix of anxiety and suspicion. We've only spoken a few times since Brando's death and even then, our conversation was both strained and cryptic. I try to sound unaffected as I press the answer button.

"Hello, Mother." I immediately hear a sigh across the line and roll my eyes heavenward.

"Julia, where have you been? I've been trying to reach you for days." Unless my phone is seriously fucked up, I haven't had any missed calls or texts from her number. Even during the brief period of my self-inflicted phone massacre, there was nothing. I'm about to bring this to her attention when she continues. "I'm sorry. I know you're busy, but I need to see you. I heard Angie was in Stone Creek spouting nonsense about the Baldonis."

I don't miss the tremble in her voice when she says the name that changed everything for both of us. It reeks of a desperation I haven't heard since that night twenty-two years ago when I overheard her speaking to my father. Whoever said ignorance was bliss is a fucking genius because there's a clear break in the story of my life that defines the woman I am today. My life before Carmine Baldoni and my life after. Although I only lived ten years in the former, the latter serves as the catalyst for every decision I make and who I surround myself with. My circle of friends is small. I have the girls and their significant others, and of course, Ben, but other than that and my professional relationships, I'm pretty closed off when it comes to anyone else. I learned years ago that the larger your circle, the greater the capacity to be crushed. At least for now, it works.

"Mother, how do you know that?" I have no idea how she knows about Angie's visit. Just as I open my mouth to question her, she interrupts.

"I have my ways darling." Of course she does. Every time something happens that involves me, she knows the details almost before I do. It's as if she has a type of telepathic link to my brain. My mouth goes dry and my heartbeat slams in my chest like a drum beating out an erratic cadence. Silence hangs between us, and for a moment, I think she may have hung up.

"Julia, this is important and certainly not something to be discussed over an unsecured line." I'm stunned. For the first time since I picked up the phone, I understand the gravity of the situation. Something is going on and I'm determined to find out what.

"Okay, Mom. I'm in Stone Creek with Ben for the week. As soon as I return to the city, I'll call you." My thoughts are spinning as I try to imagine whatever she needs to tell me that requires a face-to-face. "But, what's important enough that we can't talk now? You've never worried about an unsecured line before. What gives?"

"It's complicated, Julia. Please don't push the issue. We'll talk when you get back. But please call me as soon as you can."

"I will, Mom. I love you." She responds with the same before the line goes silent. It's true, I love my mother. She protected me for the first decade of my life from the evil that was Carmine Baldoni. She helped me escape a loveless and abusive marriage—and ensured I had what I needed to not give that bastard an heir that would tie me to him forever. But as much as I try not to, I do blame her for the things that happened under Carmine's roof. How could she not protect her only daughter from that man's evil? Although I never said anything, she wasn't blind to the kind of man my father was, and she still sent me there. That's one thing I may never know the answer to. Would it have been different if I had told her what happened there?

I did nothing wrong. It's true that monsters exist in our nightmares, and that they have faces, names, and sometimes share the same DNA as you.

"Ma'am?" I'm brought out of my walk down memory lane by the waiter, who's staring at me, obviously waiting for an answer to a question I didn't hear. Heat rushes to my cheeks as embarrassment colors my face. "I'm sorry. What did you say?"

He offers an apologetic look then continues as if I had heard him the first time. "Would you like to order now, or will Mr. King be joining you?" Will Ben join me? That's a good question. Looking at the time, I see it's been an hour since I sat down. I left him sleeping, and I'm not sure when he'll be down. As if on cue, my stomach rumbles, providing my answer. We both chuckle and I quickly recover.

"Yes, please. I'll have the pancake platter with a side of bacon and a mimosa, too. Make it a Buck's Fizz, please?" The last part comes out more like a question. Would this man judge me for tying one on so early in the day? Certainly not, but I can't quite miss his raised brow as the words leave my mouth. Before I have a chance to change my mind, he turns and makes his way to the kitchen, leaving me alone in my embarrassment.

Draining the cup of coffee, I glance up and see Ben prowling toward me all sexed up and handsome in a white button down and gray slacks. His dark brown hair is held back by a pair of aviators and he's sex personified. When he reaches the table, he bends and presses his lips softly to mine and electricity immediately shoots through me.

He takes the seat across from me, and the waiter appears, a coffee in hand, placing it on the table. "Thank you, John." He waits until the man disappears before locking eyes with me. "So, how did you sleep last night?" His mischievous grin and the way he's looking at me like I'm his next meal tells me he knows exactly how my night went.

I can't resist messing with him a little. Feigning a yawn, I lean back in my chair and toss my hair over my shoulder, revealing the evidence he left on my neck. "I've had better."

The shock on his face is priceless as he scrambles to recover from my declaration. He stares at me with a what-the-fuck expression when the corner of my mouth turns up before exploding into a full-blown grin followed by a fit of giggles. Realizing what I'm doing, his mouth curves into a smile as well. "Relax Loverboy, I think you know how I slept, and you are responsible for every sinful minute."

"You had me worried I was off my game." His eyebrows wiggle as he speaks, and once again, I feel familiar tingles spiral across my body. Before I can act on them, John returns with my plate of food. I smile as he places it in front of me and turns to Ben. "Thank you, John. I'll have the same, please."

"Yes, sir." Then he is gone.

My fingers wrap around the crystal stem of the glass as I lift it to my lips. The first sensation I taste is the burst of freshly squeezed orange juice. The flavor of citrus explodes on my tongue followed by the subtle burn from the champagne. Between this drink and the rich coffee, I'm in an alcohol and caffeine-induced heaven.

After a few minutes, Ben's breakfast is delivered, and we eat in companionable silence until his phone buzzes. Confusion coats his expression when he glances at the screen. He hesitates a moment before accepting the call. "King."

Knight speaks loud enough for me to hear. "Hey, brother. My phone broke, and I'm using a friend's. Listen, is there any way you can put me on the set list for next week? This new band could use the exposure." Ben laughs to himself and shakes his head.

"Knight, sure man. I'll get your name down. Will Friday or Saturday work better, or how about you take both nights? Molly had to cancel her Friday, so the weekend is wide open." I love it when Ben is lost in conversation with one of his brothers. The way his eyes crinkle around the corners lights up his entire face, especially when he flashes that million-dollar smile. While they continue ironing out the details of what I assume is a Knight King concert, I motion the waiter for another mimosa. Yes, the first one was strong, but I'm not driving today. In fact, I have no idea what I'm doing today until my phone signals a text message. I see it's a group chat between Tess, Lucy, and me. The message is actually from Lucy. I can't contain the laugh that bursts from my mouth when I read the text.

Lucy: "Hey Bitches, lunch today, noon at the Bluebird."

That's it, short, sweet, and hilariously to the point. Tess responds with an eye roll emoji and I send a thumbs up, turning my phone so Ben can read the text. He almost chokes on his drink when he reads the words.

"Man, Jackson is going to have his hands full with that one." This time it's my turn to choke.

After sputtering and coughing, I level my eyes at him. "You think?" Then we both break out in laughter. We finish eating and our glasses are empty when Ben and I make our way toward the lobby. After a quick kiss, we part ways. Ben, to tend to hotel business and me to entertain my two friends' crazy.

My phone buzzes and a frown washes across my face. My fingers tremble as I decline the call. A storm cloud of thoughts floods my mind and bile rises in my throat just seeing his name. Whatever venom he wants to spew can wait. Closing my eyes, I press my back against the mirrored wall, my chest heaving. I take measured breaths until my mind clears and my heart rate returns to normal. He's ruined enough of my life. I refuse to give him anymore. I'll enjoy the day with my friends before going down that road to hell. If that's where I'm headed, I'll be damned if I don't drag him along with me.

Chapter
NINE

Ben

"**B**en, did you hear what I said?" My assistant, Brenda, is staring at me like I've lost my mind and maybe I have. Ever since this shit show with Julia and her psycho family reared its ugly head, I can't concentrate on anything else. When Angie interrupted Jack and Lucy's engagement party with that announcement, it was just the beginning. And now with the possibility of her actually taking the lead in that horrific family, it's amazing I know my own name. Julia is on a collision course with her future and I'm powerless to stop it.

"I'm sorry. What did you say?"

"I said Jackson called and wants you and Julia to be at the bar at eight tonight." Remembering that conversation with my brother, I nod.

"Thanks, Brenda. Would you close the door on your way out, please?" As soon as I'm alone, I open my laptop, my eyes landing on the framed picture on my desk. Staring back at me are my loving parents. I'm instantly hit by a wall of guilt. Two of the most important people in my life. I've been so busy lately, I haven't been available for the two who would give their life for me or any of my brothers.

I grab my jacket and head for the door, pausing when Brenda gives me the side eye and grins. "I'm going out. See you later."

"Give Robert and Olivia my best." Dammit, I swear that woman has a sixth sense. I'd laugh if I wasn't so creeped out by her knowledge.

The drive to my parents' house takes twenty minutes, and I'm mesmerized by the century-old oaks that create arches hugging the sides of the cobblestone drive. I didn't grow up in Stone Creek, but my parents moved here from Michigan two years ago, which caused Jackson, Knight, and me to follow shortly after. We've each found our niche here—me at the Lux, Knight with his music store, and Jackson with his club, Jack's Place. We traded arctic temperatures and mountains of snow for crisp, clear, moderate temperatures, and I wouldn't go back for anything. Courtland, on the other hand, made his fortune in and still calls Manhattan home, and the fucker says he enjoys the Manhattan winter.

Pulling up to the traditional ranch-style house, I open the car door and slide my aviators to the top of my head. As I approach the porch, I hear the familiar laughter of my precious mother beyond the door. I raise my hand to knock when it suddenly opens to reveal her petite frame. Olivia King has always been a vision, and today is no different. She stands before me wearing white cropped pants with a red South Carolina Gamecocks sweatshirt. Her feet are bare, and her brunette hair is swept back in a low ponytail.

"Benjamin, what a surprise." Her expression turns serious and I'm suddenly wracked with guilt. She wraps her arms tightly around me, then presses her lips to my cheek. Pulling back, I see the tears gathering in her eyes before she quickly wipes them away. Something is wrong, and I'm not leaving here until I find out what it is. "Mom."

She holds up a hand and ushers me inside. "Not now, Son." She turns and leads the way into my dad's study. I follow her into the room and my heart jackhammers in my chest when I lay eyes on him. His hair is disheveled, and he's still in his pajamas as if he just rolled out of bed. Dark circles mar his pale complexion. Trying to conceal my shock, I walk over, and he looks up at me and flashes that King smile, dimples included. "Son."

"Hi, Dad. How are you feeling?" The minute the words leave my lips, I'm filled with regret. He looks like death warmed over. The last time I saw my father like this was midway through his cancer treatments. He's a survivor, he's been in remission for months. After Courtland arranged that experimental treatment in Peru last year, we just expected it to be over, but seeing him today has the fear that I try to ignore coming back tenfold.

Before he can respond, my mom quickly interrupts. "Ben, I was just about to make some sandwiches. Would you join us for lunch?" The tightness that began earlier in my throat grows into a powerful knot. After a minute, I realize I'm still rooted in my spot, and they are staring at me, concern etched on both their faces.

"I'm sorry, Mom. Of course, I'll join you for lunch. Let me help you." I know something's wrong when she doesn't reject my help. Giving my dad a wan smile, I turn, trudging behind her until we've reached the kitchen and are out of earshot of him.

She doesn't look at me as she faces the window, gazing out over the lush grassy meadow like she always does when something is troubling her. Her sad expression is reflected by the glass. I place my hands on her shoulders, and she turns but still doesn't make eye contact.

"Mom." It's all I can get out, the rest of my words getting stuck in my throat. A million thoughts are catapulting through my brain and none of them are good. He's had issues with his numbers in the past, but I've never seen him so frail.

When my mom finally speaks, her voice is almost unrecognizable. "Son. We were going to tell you, to tell all of you, but with Courtland out of the country and Knight gone…" She trails off before continuing. "Your father and I wanted you all together when we had this conversation."

This time I cut her off. "What conversation, Mom." Bitterness taints my words. I'm not angry with my mom or dad. *Fuck cancer*. My breaths are harsh, and I try to get a grip and focus on what I need to say, and what I need to know. "I'm sorry. I didn't mean to sound like I was placing blame on you. It's just, fuck."

I know it's bad when she doesn't chastise me for my choice of words. In fact, it's me who registers shock when she replies. "Yeah, fuck cancer." Olivia King, my mother, who has impeccable manners and has never uttered a curse word in her life, just dropped the F-bomb. I don't blame her at all. She drops onto the bar stool and buries her face in her hands before lifting it, wiping stray tears from her eyes.

Dragging a stool beside her, I wrap my arms around her tiny frame as sobs wrack her body and she holds on to me for dear life. I'm gutted by this unexpected turn of events. Pulling back a little, her eyes meet mine, and I suck in a ragged breath. It feels as if the proverbial elephant is sitting on my chest. "I'm here, Mom. What's going on? Tell me, please."

Hesitating, she glances over her shoulder to make sure we're still alone, and she finally speaks. "We got the call at the beginning of this week. As you know, your father's original cancer is in remission and has been for almost a year, thanks to the treatments he had in Peru." She's wringing her hands together, her eyes darting back and forth as her words come together. "Remember the scare we had about six months ago when his numbers came back high?"

I nod, still not understanding where she's going with this. "At first, the doctors said it was an infection and ordered a round of antibiotics. That appeared to have cleared it until three weeks ago when they came back high again." I'm fighting the urge to interrupt her, but I need to know everything she's willing to share.

When she stops talking, I encourage her to continue. She sniffles and releases a big breath. "The doctor immediately placed him on another regimen of antibiotics but after two weeks, the numbers were higher than ever. They performed a couple of other tests and when they tested his bone marrow, that's when they found it." Oh God, this is worse than I expected. She shakes her head, and I see the tears she's holding back. "Apparently, this multiple myeloma has been there all along and the other cancer was masking it, making it virtually undetectable until now."

I see her speaking, but all I can hear is white noise with a few phrases filtering through. "My God." "It's serious this time, Ben." What is she saying? Cancer is serious, and we almost lost him, but if we're having this conversation and she is this wrecked, the situation must be different.

"Yes, Mom, I know it's serious, just like last time." I'm waiting for her to agree, but when she looks at me, her face gaunt, and she frowns, I know.

"It's terminal," I say so she doesn't have to give voice to the two words that have haunted me since he was first diagnosed. My strong mother doesn't speak again, just nods her head and mouths, "yes." She falls into my arms again.

We stay that way until she pulls back, glancing at the sandwich fixings on the counter behind her. Knowing we've spent a suspicious amount of time in the kitchen with no lunch to prove it, I dive in, spreading mayonnaise on bread, before layering it with ham, turkey, lettuce, and tomato. While I'm doing this, she gets three glasses from the cupboard, fills them with ice, then retrieves the pitcher of sweet tea from the refrigerator.

We place everything on a serving tray, and I carry it to the dining table. My father is already sitting there, looking more haggard than when I walked in. My eyes roam nervously between them as my mom and I take our seats on either side of him.

The silence is unimaginable, and the tension is so thick, I'm not sure if even the sharpest knife could cut it. Nausea rolls through me in waves as I sit with my head lowered, unable to meet his gaze. I take two bites of my sandwich then drop it on my plate, suddenly averse to adding anything else to my mouth, for fear of it making a return appearance.

Mom and Dad are attempting to make light conversation, and with every word, I feel my jaw clench more tightly and my hands ball into tighter fists. I'm on the edge of exploding when my father clears his throat and levels me with his gaze. "Benjamin, I know your mother spoke to you. That you're aware I'm sick again, and this time it's different." I sit with my jaw hanging as his words wash over me like a tidal wave, destroying everything in its path. It's one thing to hear the news from my mother, but it's surreal when he utters the words. "I hope you know we weren't trying to keep this from you. We were just waiting until you boys could be here together. Since you stopped by and caught us off guard, we had to tell you."

All I can do is nod at this point. Of course, this isn't the type of news to be shared through text or a phone call, and since they just found out this week, there hasn't been time to get us together.

Leaning back in the chair, my hands clasped together on the table, I look at my dad. Really look in his eyes. I've avoided them since I walked in and now it's like I'm seeing him for the first time. The same navy eyes he shares with Courtland have a look of exhaustion I've never seen before today. The deathlike pallor of his face makes me notice wrinkles that weren't there a few weeks ago.

We finish our lunch in uncomfortable silence, and I manage to get in a few more bites before pushing my plate away. My purpose for coming here today was to get their perspective on this Julia business, but it quickly became clear that it could wait. Whatever happens between the two of us, we'll have to handle it on our own.

After I help my mother clear the table, I say my goodbyes. I tell them I have hotel business to attend to, when in reality I need to put some distance between myself and my parents. If not, I will completely fall apart.

Driving away from their house, I feel like I've been sucker punched. My heart beats erratically and I can't seem to get enough oxygen to my lungs. I pull over to the shoulder before I lose consciousness and try to get my breathing under control. When my breaths are manageable, my fingers punch in the familiar number. The call goes to voicemail. I wait for the dreaded beep to speak, trying to hide the shake in my voice.

"Hello Sunshine. I just wanted to remind you we're meeting Jack tonight. Anyway, have fun with the girls. I'll pick you up around seven-thirty." Ending the call, I toss my phone to the passenger seat. I sit, a plethora of thoughts running rampant, before I grab my phone again and make the call. I'm not sure if it's my place, but he's my twin—half of me. He picks up on the second ring.

"Hey, little bro." I can hear his smirk over the line.

"Hey, Court. We have to talk. You need to come home now."

I hang up before he can object and then peel onto the road, testing the speed limit as this recent news is testing my limits.

Chapter TEN

Julia

As soon as I enter the Bluebird, I hear the unmistakable shriek of Lucy Dawson, soon-to-be Lucy King, echoing off the low acoustics of the cinderblock walls.

"Oh my God, Julia, get your ass back here." She waves down a waitress, who skitters to our table, three menus in hand. Placing them in front of us, she stands looking expectantly at me.

I stare back in confusion until it registers that she's waiting for my drink order. "Um, what are you guys drinking?" Lucy lets out a very Lucy-like burp, then speaks without missing a beat.

"What else, Jules? Cosmos." I should have guessed. That's been our go-to drink since our days at Juilliard.

Shaking my head, I nod toward the empty glasses. "Bring me a Cosmo, I guess."

"Hell, yeah." Lucy snorts.

"So, Julia, what's going on?" Tess blinks her big blue eyes as she takes a sip of her drink, and Lucy sits with her arms folded across her chest like a drill sergeant. I lean back and settle in for the interrogation

I've been expecting. Lucky for me, the waitress delivers my drink, and I immediately take a rather big gulp, looking at my glass to avoid their stares. I'm waiting for one of them to speak, but they both continue waiting for me to start. Taking a deep breath and releasing a sigh, I set my glass down.

"So, what do you want to know?" Tess knows a little about my situation, but I haven't had an all-out chickfest with Lucy yet.

"Anything you feel comfortable sharing." Tess's words are empathetic. She's had her fair share of family issues, so she understands how traumatic those conversations can be. Lucy, on the other hand, has dealt with a different set of family problems. Namely, her single-minded controlling mother, but she still craves the chaos a good conflict creates.

I'm about to open my mouth when the waitress comes to take our food orders. We decide on the chef salads and Bottomless Cosmos. We have a lot to catch up on, and if I'm going down that road today, I'm going to need all the liquid courage I can get. I drain my glass and turn my eyes toward my friends.

"I'll give you the abbreviated version because there aren't enough hours left in the day for the long version." My friends don't speak. I'm not sure if they don't know what to say or if they're giving me space to talk. Whatever the reason, I'm grateful for their silence.

"My father was absent from my life until I was ten years old. That's when Carmine Baldoni entered the picture. I started visiting him and those visits continued until I was seventeen." Reaching for my glass, I take a sip, allowing the citrusy burn to linger on my tongue before swallowing. Tess's eyes shine with tears, but Lucy looks like she wants to murder someone.

She knows firsthand the lengths the Baldonis will go to get retribution. This was clear when she and I were taken earlier this year.

Thankfully, Ben and Jackson saved our lives, and in the process, Brando was killed, but it didn't end there.

Angie was the one who told me about the will right after she dropped the bombshell, and apparently since I was the second child born to Carmine, I am next in line to run the family business. At first, I was in total opposition, but after relaying yesterday's conversation with Angie to Ben and my mother, we knew the alternative was Danny, Joey, or Angie. But Danny gets off on violence in any form, and Joey and Angie—like me, want no part of it. I'm still not sure what the next move is, but one thing is certain, as much as I want distance from this family, I can't let it fall into Danny's hands.

They both sit in stunned silence as our food arrives. Clearing my throat, I swallow; my mouth suddenly feels like cotton. Grabbing my glass, I take another healthy gulp before continuing. "I'm sorry I didn't tell either of you what was going on. Like I said, I tried to break ties with the family. Anyway, can you forgive me for keeping that part of my life hidden?" I conveniently leave out the fact I'm married. Even though I told Molly in a moment of distress, I can't risk endangering anyone else.

It's Lucy who speaks next. "Oh my God, Jules, you have nothing to be sorry about. I only got a small glimpse of their evil when we were kidnapped, but if I had endured what I'm sure was a horrific childhood with those monsters, I would have done the same or worse." She reaches over and takes my hand in hers. I look at Tess, who has tears streaming down her cheeks. Grabbing her hand with my free one, I bring it to my lips and brush it with a light kiss.

We sit unmoving for several minutes before we're brought back to the moment by a faint ringing. Realizing it's my phone in my bag, I grab it. But when I see the number displayed, my hand freezes for just a moment before I tap decline. Looking back at my friends and seeing the sympathetic looks on their faces, I know it's time to change the subject. "Enough of sad sack Julia. Lucy, tell me what's going on with the wedding planning?" She offers a weak smile, but I think she knows this is what I need.

"Oh, you know, Jackson shoots down every idea I have, so it's only fair I reciprocate." The three of us laugh at her declaration. Their enemies-to-lovers courtship has kept them on their toes.

"Lucy, I think asking the President of the United States to perform the ceremony is a little over the top, don't you?" I had heard this rumor, but I want her to confirm it.

"It's not the president. It's the Secretary of State and it's not ridiculous, as Satan put it. He's a friend of a friend's third cousin." She stops abruptly and bursts out in a fit of giggles, which quickly becomes contagious, and we find ourselves unable to catch our breath. When she finally gets control, she relents. "Okay, I guess when I say it out loud, it sounds a little over the top. But don't tell Jackson. I want to see him squirm for a few more weeks." Tess and I make the zipper motion across our lips, showing our solidarity with her continued Lucy/Jackson crazy antics.

We finish our lunch and drinks just as my phone shows a text message. Groaning, I focus on the screen, seeing my sister's name flash across the display.

Angie: Why aren't you answering Danny's calls? You can't avoid this forever.

I shove my phone in my bag, trying to show no emotion in front of my friends. I've just spilled word vomit all over them. I think that's enough for one day.

After a few more minutes, I hug them goodbye and say that I'll see them later at Jack's Place. When I walk out, the sunshine is like a cozy blanket warming my soul. It's a gorgeous day with cotton candy clouds dotting the bright blue sky, and I make the quick decision to walk to the Lux.

When I get back to the hotel, Ben's office door is closed so I head straight to the suite. Lifting the keycard to the panel, the lock clicks open, and I walk in. I stop in my tracks when a figure comes into focus across the room. There, sitting like an intimidating god, is my brother, Danny. He's holding a glass of amber liquid. A tie hangs loosely around his neck as if he's gotten comfortable after waiting for something or, in this case, someone.

"What are you doing here, Danny? You better hope Ben doesn't see you." I'd ask him how he got in, but I doubt I really want to know. When his eyes meet mine, a smirk forms on his face. I've seen this same cold, unfeeling expression on both my father and Brando's faces, but that was long ago when I was just a scared teen.

I watch as he slowly brings the glass to his mouth like he's got all the time in the world. If Ben knew he was here now, Danny'd be a dead man.

"You won't take my calls, Julia Bear. What's a brother to think?" Cold chills run down my spine when he calls me the nickname he gave me years ago. "Besides, maybe we need to invite Loverboy to the party. I'm sure he'd want to hear all about your marriage."

There's a muffled whooshing sound inside my ears and my blood turns to ice. "You didn't answer my question. What do you want? Why are you here?" My voice shakes, but I will myself to not show distress. He drains the glass before slamming it so hard on the table it's a miracle it doesn't shatter. I jump at the sudden intrusion, my heart accelerating. The room starts spinning, and I can't catch my breath as he remains seated, glaring at me like a predator to prey.

Looking at his watch like he's bored, he speaks. "I'll cut to the chase, big sis. Five years ago, the Kings took something from our family. Now it's time to get it back." I'm looking at him, confusion clouding my brain.

"What the fuck are you talking about, Danny?" He continues glaring at me like I'm supposed to know what he's talking about. When I don't make a move to speak, he finally laughs and continues.

"You really don't know? Well, let me enlighten you, Julia Bear. It seems like your boyfriend…" He says the endearment like poison in his mouth, and my eyes widen. "He was involved in a fatal car wreck. A young woman named Leah was killed. Loverboy insisted it was an accident, but Leah was Angie's best friend—so," he nods once, "she was family. And you know what happens to those who cross the family. So when certain… shall we say… evidence? was found, Brando aided in the cover-up in exchange for Jackson King's future services to the family."

I'm paralyzed by what he's saying. I knew there was some sort of history involving Jackson, but to hear this news ignites a firestorm of emotions. "You're lying. Jackson and Ben would never agree to something like that."

He continues as if I hadn't spoken. "You wouldn't know because you were running away from your obligations. They agreed because the evidence would have been enough to convict your boyfriend." He pauses to chuckle. "We are very good at what we do. However, it seems the terms and conditions changed once Brando's death was confirmed." I'm still looking at him, not understanding where this conversation is headed until he gets to the point.

"Of course, the deal was for Jackson King to serve our family in any capacity we deemed fit and if Brando was alive, Ben would be protected. That changed when our brother died, especially since Ben King was the one who pulled the trigger." I'm suddenly struck with an awareness that I will not like where this is going.

"What does that mean, exactly?"

"It means, dear sister, as the Bible so eloquently puts it, an eye for an eye, a life for a life. It's time to collect the debt. Ben King must die."

My face pales. "Excuse me, what did you just say?" My eyes shoot daggers at the man sitting across from me. The man who terrorized and traumatized me for half my teenage years.

"I didn't stutter, Julia Bear." His cold dark eyes bore into mine, as nausea claws its way up my throat, the taste like acid on my tongue.

"You can't be serious, Danny." My eyes are wide, and the room spins.

"As a heart attack, big sis." I watch his face, searching for any sign of indecision, but he's an impenetrable fortress. Suddenly, his expression changes and an evil smirk spreads across his face.

"Julia, the beauty of it is, that you, dear sister, being the boss, hold the power to issue the decree. Are you willing to risk having all your secrets exposed by reneging on your responsibilities?" His wicked chuckle has goose bumps erupting over my body. Panic saturates my nerves as my breaths become erratic, and my heart is pumping rapidly, yet everything around me seems to stop.

"After the 'accident', Jackson was offered protection in exchange for his services, which you know extended to Ben by default and our brother's good nature." I roll my eyes at that absurdity. If Brando Baldoni or any of Carmine Baldoni's other spawns had a good-natured bone in their body, then I'm the Princess of Wales.

"Anyway, as long as our father and Brando were breathing, that deal was solid. Now with Brando out of the picture, the dirty work of the family falls to you."

"And if I refuse? Then what, Danny? I am the boss, after all." This is insanity. I'll never agree to this. I'll put a bullet between each of my siblings' eyes first or die trying.

"There's always a fail-safe in place for bleeding hearts like yourself. Make no mistake, it will be done, Julia, with or without your permission." He stands, moving toward the door, while I remain seated in the high-back chair I fell into when he started this insane story. I don't look at him as he glides past me, but I feel his dark presence and his progress is marked by the fading sounds of his footsteps. Just as he reaches the door, he calls back to me, more poison dripping from his mouth.

"You've got forty-eight hours to decide. No worries if you're not up to the challenge. We'll get it handled." I hear the door open on a creak and then close quietly behind him, leaving me wondering what the fuck just happened and how the fuck I'll make it right.

Chapter
ELEVEN

Ben

A million scenarios command my thoughts when I disconnect the call. I know he'll have a barrage of questions, the least of which is why I demanded he come home. Not to Manhattan. To Stone Creek. My home, not his. I barely make it another mile before my phone rings. This time, it's Jackson. I roll my eyes heavenward and drag in a deep breath. Swallowing hard, I press the green button.

"Hey, Jack." There's a brief pause, then his voice comes through the Bluetooth in my car.

"What the fuck, Ben? You can't just summon Courtland to Stone Creek like you're ordering an Uber or some shit." I hear his huff of aggravation over the phone. It didn't take my twin long to tattle to our brother.

"Are you finished little brother?" I make sure to keep my voice controlled when I speak. I can't afford to lose it with him now. Another pause.

I'm getting ready to make another offhand comment when he continues. "Look, he called me."

I cut him off. "You don't say?" When he doesn't reply, I take that as my cue to get to the point. "I can't get into it over the phone, but this is important. Everyone needs to be in Stone Creek together. The sooner the better. The last thing I want to do is issue demands, but you know how things are with Courtland. If you give him a choice in the matter, you'll end up regretting it."

"You're right about that, Ben, but if this family get together has anything to do with Julia and her evil empire, I don't get why it involves all of us." If he only knew. As bad as that situation is, that's not the worst thing happening right now.

"No, it has nothing to do with Julia." My voice breaks at the end, and I try to quickly cover it with a muffled cough, but he knows something's up.

When his voice comes back through, it's quieter. "Ben, what's going on?"

Taking a couple more deep breaths, I offer the only thing I can. "Jackson, do you trust me?"

Indignation coats his next words. "What the hell, Ben? After everything we've been through, how dare you ask such a thing?"

"Hey don't get defensive. I know you do. That's why I need you to understand where I'm coming from now. We'll have that conversation when everyone gets here."

He finally relents. "Okay. About tonight."

"We'll be there at eight." With that, I hang up as I'm pulling into my parking space at the hotel. Not sure if Julia's still with the girls, I head straight to my office, needing to do some research of my own.

Brenda looks up from her computer and gives me a bright smile. As I reach the door, I call over my shoulder. "Hold my calls, please." I see her nod as I disappear behind the dark mahogany door.

Settling at my desk, my eyes wander to the antique bookcase across the room, landing on several framed photos of my family at various stages from our past. My favorite is the one of all of us sitting in a field of wildflowers, Mom and Dad in the middle, my brothers and me crowded around them.

I'm not sure how long I sit looking at their smiling faces encased in glass and wood before turning my attention to the computer screen, my fingers flying furiously over the keys. It only takes a few seconds for the search to pull up.

> *Multiple Myeloma: an uncommon blood cancer that affects bone marrow, the body's blood-forming system.*
>
> *Prognosis: Some people live ten years or more. Early detection is key to life expectancy. Seventy-eight percent of people are alive five years after being diagnosed.*
>
> *Symptoms of late-stage MM: feeling very tired, losing a lot of weight, not feeling like eating, bruising or bleeding easily...*

I stop reading after the first four symptoms because they perfectly describe Dad. Fuck, this can't be happening. Scrubbing a hand across my face, I close the search and turn my attention to the floor-to-ceiling window, through which I can see the sabal palms swaying gently in the wind, creating a portrait of rich earth tones against a gray sky.

Reaching for my phone, I pull up her number and hit call. It immediately goes to voicemail, which is odd, except I guess it's not when she's immersed in a sea of gossip with Lucy and Tess. I forgo leaving a message and tap out a text instead.

Me: Hey, Sunshine, I hope you're enjoying your lunch with the girls. Just call me when you are free. No rush.

I toss my phone across the desk. Everything's fine. Dad will be okay, and Julia is safe here. Her family doesn't know she's in Stone Creek.

Grabbing my phone again, I hammer out a group text to my brothers. I hate to disrupt whatever they have going on but I'm sure when the news comes to light, all my brothers will be grateful we are together. Well, maybe grateful isn't the correct word, but at least they won't be alone and in the dark.

> Me: Hey guys, something big has come up. I can't get into it now, but I can tell you that we all need to be in Stone Creek together soon. So, whatever can be canceled or postponed please make the necessary arrangements. If it wasn't important, I wouldn't ask. Let me know when you'll be here.

I leave my office and head for the bar. My expression must not hide my feelings because as soon as I reach the bar, Gus slides a glass of amber liquid in front of me. Raising it in salute, I swallow it in one long gulp and ask for another. He shakes his head and chuckles deeply as he takes the glass from my grasp.

After he hands me the second drink and I turn to leave, he calls to me. "Hey boss." I'm aggravated and don't want to talk. I stop, but don't turn toward his voice. Whatever he's going to say, he can say to my back.

"What is it, Gus?" I toss over my shoulder. I'm sure he can sense the irritation in my voice.

"Is she worth it?" He correctly assumes my frustration is because of a woman. But he doesn't know Julia—if he did, he'd know how foolish his question is. I can't help the laugh that spills from my mouth.

"She's worth everything." With that, I stride back to my office, closing the door behind me.

Chapter
TWELVE

Ben

It's seven-thirty when I pull up at Jack's Place. Everyone will be here at eight. Well, Jackson and the girls, minus Molly. Courtland and Knight messaged me saying they would be back tomorrow, but that's not soon enough. While they're off doing whatever they do, I'm here handling this fuck show. I can't blame them for living their lives, though, and I need to get my head on straight before facing my brother tonight. I feel as though I'm choking as I pull at the collar of my Henley.

Getting out of my car, I push through the door and head straight for the bar. There's a new bartender working tonight. I don't bother learning names anymore. Jackson blows through employees like he does bourbon. It's unbelievable—I mean, with his dazzling personality, who wouldn't want to work for him? I laugh to myself and order my usual Macallan neat, then head to the table in the back.

I bring the glass to my lips, inhaling the sherry forward notes along with subtle leather. Taking a sip, I allow the flavors to settle on my tongue before swallowing, the slow burn sliding down my throat. I'm sitting with my head thrown back against the high back leather chair when I hear their voices—Tess's normal tones and Lucy's unmistakable screech, coming straight toward me. Following closely behind is my brother. I hardly notice them slide boisterously into three chairs. The one thing I do notice is the absence of the only woman I want to see tonight. "Where the hell is Julia?" I can't help my biting tone.

"Hey, good to see you too, Ben." Tess snaps back, but when she sees my expression, she softens. "She isn't here? I thought for sure she would beat us." I vaguely register her words as I grab my phone and stab at her number. I haven't seen her since breakfast this morning, and when she didn't answer earlier, I chalked it up to being busy with the girls. It goes to voicemail after one ring.

"Have you talked to her since lunch?" I'm trying to rein in the panic creeping in, but it's damn hard when everyone is staring at me like they're waiting for the punchline. Lucy is the one to break the stare down first.

"Relax, Ben. I'm sure she's just running late. Her phone probably died or something. Don't worry so much. She's a big girl." Her laugh is meant to make me feel better, but it's doing just the opposite.

I should have checked the room before leaving my office, but I thought she was riding with one of the girls. A dozen scenarios play out before my eyes, and I have an unsettling feeling in my gut that something is very wrong. I'm ready to go to the hotel, when I see her strolling through the door. My entire body relaxes as relief washes over me like a hundred waterfalls cascading into unknown depths. My steps eat up the distance between us, and I immediately pull her into a tight embrace. My lips find hers, and I take her in a furious kiss that leaves us both gasping for air.

"God, Sunshine, you scared the shit out of me. Where have you been?" It sounds like an accusation, and when she flinches at my rough tone, my heart stammers. Grabbing both her shoulders, I stare deep into her dark brown eyes. "I'm sorry, it's just, I couldn't reach you. With everything going on, I was beginning to think the worst."

She rests her head against my chest, not looking at me when she speaks. "I'm sorry I worried you. Let's talk when we get back to the room, okay?" Tilting her chin up so I can read her face, I notice the tear stains on her cheeks. Her eyes are red, swollen, and filled with something that looks like fear.

My chest clenches and my face turns to stone. "Who do I need to kill?"

"It's just been a long day. I'm fine. Please, we'll talk later." Her eyes are pleading, and as much as I want answers, I won't push. Not right now.

"Okay." I let my arms fall to my sides and turn back toward where our friends wait.

"I just need a minute. I'll meet you at the table." I watch her disappear to the ladies' room before I wander back to our group. I can't shake this feeling in my gut there's something she isn't telling me. As much as I want to chase her, she made it clear we would talk later, and I need to respect that. It's hard with so many secrets floating around. One thing is certain. Whatever has her rattled is enough for her to arrive late, and I'd stake my last dollar it has something to do with that sick son of a bitch, Danny. I grab my drink and drain it in one go. I hold up the glass, motioning for another. I don't want to get shit faced, but whatever's going on with Julia has me on edge, so a few whiskeys may be necessary to get through tonight.

The purpose of this meeting is to discuss the re-grand opening of Jack's Place. He had one grand opening, but according to him and the residents of Stone Creek, anytime there's a remodel to a business it's followed by a re-grand opening. Whatever floats your boat. I remind myself to make sure the owner of the hotel I manage doesn't plan to make any major renovations any time soon.

We spend the next two hours planning, discussing, and calculating every single detail before a wide yawn splits Julia's face. Everyone laughs and we take that as our cue to leave.

"Well, guys, it's been real." I've been able to avoid the questioning looks Jackson has thrown my way all night, so when we stand to leave, relief sweeps over me. Tomorrow we'll all be together. Everyone will find out soon enough that Dad is sick again. There's no need to dash hopes until necessary.

The drive back to the Lux is tense, and neither of us speaks. I steal glances at her, looking for any indication she's ready to talk, but her expression gives nothing away. My chest tightens and I feel something wet forming in the corner of my eyes. The usual ease of our conversation is thwarted by whatever she's holding back. It's like we're encased in glass. The slightest noise would cause us to shatter. We walk to the suite, our hands occasionally brushing but not lingering. The closer we get to the door, the faster my heart jackhammers in my chest. My breathing becomes erratic and the lump forming in my stomach turns into a boulder as Julia walks ahead of me.

When the door closes behind us, I go to the love seat, sagging into the plush cushions to wait for her. It's not long before she's sitting in a chair opposite me. I need to find out what's plaguing her, but before thinking better of it, I blurt out my news.

"My dad's sick again." My eyes hold her gaze as the color drains from her face. She moves from the chair to the spot next to me. She rests her head on my shoulder as I wrap my arms around her, pulling her into a gentle hug. She doesn't say anything, just sits in my arms like she's trying to infuse some of her strength into me. After a few quiet moments, I find the strength to speak. When I open my mouth, the floodgates burst and all my anguish spills out. "He and Mom received the news earlier this week, but they told me this afternoon. The doctors are giving him a few months at most."

Suddenly my mind clears, and I remember I'm not the only one hurting tonight. Leaning forward, I turn toward her. "Sunshine, you said we'd talk when we got back, So, tell me. What happened?" She inhales a deep breath, then releases it just as deeply.

"It's not important. It can wait. Tonight, I'm here for you, Ben. Let me be here for you, please." She moves to my lap, straddling me. The heat of her center lands squarely between my legs. Her lips touch mine in a trembling kiss that quickly turns feral. I need her, and she needs me. I need to forget, and she's the only one who can give me that. We'll forget together.

Chapter

THIRTEEN

Julia

Iwake up to something warm and hard pressed against my backside. I smile, pushing back against him seductively. Last night was a fever dream, or at least it felt like one. We became a mix of arms and legs tangled in erotic pleasure. After hearing the news of his dad's illness, he needed the release, and God knows I did too. But today's a new day. It all comes flooding back with devastating clarity. Danny's visit. His threats and demands leave me grappling with reality.

I didn't spend almost a decade in hell to become weak now. Danny and Joey have always underestimated me and now is not the time for my resolve to crumble. Sliding carefully out of bed, I pull on my terry cloth robe and make my way across the room. Closing the bedroom door behind me, I amble to the loveseat, sit and pull my legs underneath me. Picking up my phone, I decide to try again to get answers. After two rings, her beautiful face comes into view.

"Hi, Mom." I keep my voice low and my expression neutral. I need her advice, but I don't need her going ballistic every time I'm in distress. She will know soon enough the severity of the situation.

"Julia, I'm glad you called. Are you back in the city?" I swallow the rising nausea.

"No, Mom, we're still in Stone Creek, but I need to talk to you, and it couldn't wait." I hear her sharp intake of breath and know she's about to go into full Mama Bear mode when I cut her off. "Look, I just need to ask you a question."

"Okay, Julia. What do you need to know?"

"You know I'll be forever grateful you got me away from Michael, and I haven't heard from him in years. I need to know. Is there a chance he'll come back for me?"

"Where is this coming from, Julia?"

"Mom, I'm afraid Danny's going to tell Ben things that I really should tell him myself—but I'm just not ready. I also know your parents died when you were a teenager, and I can't help thinking the two may be connected. What can you tell me about them?" Her deep sigh lets me know she doesn't want to talk about them. Every time she wants to avoid a conversation, she sighs. I glance at the bedroom door, ensuring I'm still alone. Until I have answers, there's no reason to burden him with premature consternation.

"This is important, Mom. Danny came to see me yesterday."

"He went to Stone Creek? Oh my God, Julia, what did he say?" Now it's my turn to go silent. "Tell me Julia." There's an urgency that I rarely hear. I clear my throat and steel myself for what comes next.

"He's still pressuring me about taking over the family business and he's taunting me about my marriage to Michael. I basically told him to go fuck himself."

"Language, darling." I snort at her words.

"Please, Mom. My potty mouth is the least of my worries."

"So, what are you going to do?" *What am I going to do?* Whenever I consider my options, I literally become sick to my stomach. Just thinking about Danny and his demands has my blood boiling.

"I'm not sure at this point. He's making threats, but I can't help but think something has him running scared. It's been six months since Brando was killed. Why now? I need to find some way to placate him without completely giving in to his demands. That's the reason I'm asking about your parents. You've never told me much about them, just that your father held a lot of power in the city. I thought maybe there were some connections we could use to gain the upper hand, and given that you were involved with Carmine, I was hoping maybe you had some intelligence that could give me an advantage." I see a flash of something in her eyes before it disappears.

"Oh, Julia, I don't know anything that could help you. There are things I will tell you when the time is right. Until then, I need you to trust me." Before I can question her, the bedroom door opens, and I turn my attention to the gorgeous man standing there. I can't tear my eyes away from his chiseled good looks and that delicious V pointing to the promised land below the waistband of his joggers. I say a quick goodbye to my mother, promising we'll get together as soon as I'm back in town.

By the time I end the call, he's leaning over my chair, his hands resting on the arms, caging me in as his salacious gaze rakes over my body. I release a breath and my body visibly relaxes when I realize he didn't hear my conversation with my mother. His lips brush mine in a lazy kiss. He's taking his time, savoring my mouth.

"Good morning, Sunshine." His eyes never stray from mine. The way he is looking at me, his eyes the color of expensive brandy, does little to steel my nerves. It's like he's looking into my soul and can see every crack and scar that's hiding there. Heat radiates across my cheeks and flows down my entire body.

"Hi." His dark hair hangs across his forehead, damp from the shower, making him appear younger than his thirty-nine years. Ink crawls down his biceps and punctuates his wrists. Hard muscles define his stomach, and I carefully run my fingers along them in broad strokes, committing the feel to memory.

Remembering last night has me pressing my thighs together, the pressure building up, begging for a release. He must sense my predicament because he chuckles to himself and cocks his head to the side, giving me that dimpled smile. "Are you okay, Sunshine?" Swallowing my desire, I clear my throat.

"Sure, I'm fine. It's just, you know. Thinking about last night." I blush at the thought of the way we enjoyed each other's bodies. He pulls me up and presses his length against me as I rest my head on his broad chest, breathing in his masculine scent. Sandalwood and spice—all Ben King. I could stay like this indefinitely, tucked away from the world and everything related to secret marriages and the Baldoni family.

I never took that name, even after my father entered the picture. Even when he insisted, I clung to the Bernard name, the only name I knew, the name my mother chose for me. I never understood why my mother gave me her mother's maiden name instead of her own, and every time I asked, she skirted the question. Eventually, it became a moot point.

After a few minutes, I step out of his arms, noticing the time. Moving to the desk, I grab my laptop, firing it up as Ben retreats to the bedroom. I should get dressed, do something productive. And I need to check in with the studio since I'll be away all week. But first, this gnawing sensation in the back of my mind won't let me rest. My fingers fly across the keys, and I press enter. Unfortunately, my search ends as quickly as it began.

Katherine Tolliver. My mother. I see the generic information. Information I already know. I'm not sure what I expected to find, but maybe a few more nuggets to add to what I already have. Disappointment clouds my vision as I close out that tab and open a new one. Pulling up my email, there's nothing new. The studio is in good hands, but I'm antsy just sitting here. Ben has meetings today, so I decide to do some small-town shopping.

After leaving the suite, I text Tess while I wait for the Uber to collect me. I'll swing by Knight's music store and pick her up, then we'll hit the town together.

She's outside, reaching for the door handle, before the car comes to a full stop. I can't help the laugh that bubbles from my mouth when she slides in beside me. "God, Tess, one would think you haven't been shopping in months." She shoots me a warning glare before giggling as she pushes her hair over one shoulder. Her sapphire eyes are dancing with mirth.

"Considering I've been working non-stop these last few weeks while Knight's been mostly gone, I haven't seen the inside of a boutique in about that long. My shopping gene is about to call for a mutiny." We both laugh.

We decide to check out a new boutique that just recently opened a few miles outside of Stone Creek. We're both lost in our phones, checking out the store's website, when I hear the first pop. "Get down." Instinct has me pushing Tess to the floor and hovering over her body. A round of successive shots pierces the air outside the car.

The driver swerves, and Tess screams, fear and shock lacing her cries. I remain silent, anger driving my emotions, as the car begins to pick up speed. Peering over the seat, I notice the driver is slumped forward. He's been hit, his foot wedged against the accelerator. The three of us are at the mercy of the road. There's a small glass partition separating the front seat from us. I feel a small give when I push against it, but not enough to break through the barrier. After multiple attempts to break the partition, I give up and wrap my body around hers and brace for impact.

Everything happens in slow motion. I'm leaning over Tess, whose body is convulsing with fear as she screams. All I can think of is my sweet Ben and how much I love him. Why didn't I say it more? He deserves to know how I feel. Before I can dwell on our fate, I feel the car become airborne. My scream joins Tess's as I sense the vehicle plummeting. Falling, falling—it feels like we fall forever before the car crashes back to earth. When it jolts to a stop, everything fades to black.

Chapter
FOURTEEN

Ben

"Slow down, Jackson. What?" Panic courses through my veins.

"There's been an accident. I picked it up on the scanner at the bar." Of course, he has a police scanner. I don't wait for him to continue.

"Who's involved? Was anyone hurt? What happened?" My mind races to everyone in my family, making a mental calculation of everyone's whereabouts.

"I don't know for sure. It happened a few miles outside the city limits." Relief takes over as I remember that Julia and Tess are out shopping, but they usually keep to the local shops. Before I formulate an appropriate response, my phone beeps with an incoming call.

"Hey, it's Julia. I need to take this." My heart feels like it could literally beat out of my chest, so I take a deep breath to calm myself before I talk to her. "Julia, is everything okay?"

"How did you know?" Her voice sounds small. I've never heard her sound so defeated before.

"How did I know what? I was just on the phone with Jackson. He was telling me there'd been an accident, but I didn't get any details."

"This wasn't an accident, Ben. Someone shot at us. The driver was hit."

My blood turns to ice and I begin rattling off questions, desperate to keep her talking because I know if I can hear her, she's alright, at least physically. "What happened? Are you okay?"

Background noise captures my attention. Sirens and horns invade the air. I hear them getting louder as they get closer. I can hear the strain in her voice as she tries to speak louder to be heard over the approaching vehicles.

"I'm okay. We both are. Tess is pretty shaken up." I'm surprised by how calm she sounds.

My phone pings with a text and I see that Jackson has sent the location of the accident. Thank fuck.

"I'm on my way." I'm fumbling with my keys, dropping them twice before I'm able to make it to my car. I break at least a dozen laws, but I can't get there fast enough. My movements are in slow motion as hundreds of scenarios race through my mind. Until I lay hands on her, my anxiety level will continue to be off the charts. My car weaves in and out of traffic and my heart is pumping rapidly when I round the corner. I'm on an emotional rollercoaster as thoughts of my loved ones play across my mind. It's a highlight reel of my life and the people I love. My father's illness sits front and center, along with my sweet Julia.

Flashing red lights appear ahead of me long before I see the crumpled car being lifted from a ravine. My heart pounds faster the closer I get. I see two ambulances, a firetruck, and two cop cars as I scan the crowd that's gathered, searching for dark hair and chocolate eyes. I barely get the car into park before I'm rushing into the crowd. The door of one ambulance is propped open, and I see her sitting in the back with a blanket wrapped around her shoulders. She has one arm around Tess, but that's not the first thing that grabs my attention. It's the bandage covering her forehead and the jagged gash that runs from her elbow to her wrist. A paramedic is examining her arm as I make my way toward her. She turns to look at me as I reach the vehicle.

"Ben, you came." I laugh at her statement. Doesn't she know nothing could keep me away from her?

"Oh, Sunshine, you're hurt." I'm reaching for her when she melts into my arms. Tucking her into my chest, I rub my hands down her back as quiet sobs fill the air. It's enough to bring me to my knees.

"I'm sorry, Ben."

"Julia, don't apologize." My eyes catch movement beside us. Her brown eyes widen as we watch first responders carry a blanket-covered stretcher up the side of the embankment. When one man makes eye contact, I raise a questioning brow. He responds by sadly shaking his head. The driver didn't survive the accident.

Tess doesn't have any visible injuries. I'm sure Julia took the brunt of the impact by using her body as a shield during the worst of everything. I consider the possibility of a very different outcome, one that became a reality for the poor bastard driving the car.

Another bandage is secured to Julia's injured arm, and I watch as she shakes her head in response to a question. Leaning closer, I ask him to repeat what he asked. The paramedic wants the girls to be checked out at the ER, and the police are waiting for answers to their questions, too. Julia and Tess are both adamant they do not need a hospital. I'm not in agreement with their medical assessment, and I try to convince them to get checked out. After Julia gives me another 'hell no' look, I decide I won't win this battle. But I will watch over her for the next, however many hours necessary, to make sure she recovers.

After another hour and a promise to take full responsibility for the two women, the first responders relent, allowing waivers to be signed and permitting us to be on our way. It takes a little more to convince the officers to conduct their questioning at the Lux instead of the station.

It's quiet on the drive back to the hotel. Tess is still shaking, while Julia is eerily calm. Everyone processes trauma differently, and who am I to dictate what that process should look like?

When we pull up to the valet station, neither woman makes a move. Climbing out, I hand the attendant my keys and open the back door. Julia slides out willingly, but Tess is glued to the dark leather interior. Two women, two very different reactions to the events of the morning. Julia reaches her hand to Tess, who reluctantly takes it, scooting to the door and allowing Julia to pull her to a standing position. I watch as the two women walk arm in arm, drawing strength from each other. I open the door and step aside for them to enter. It's only a matter of minutes before two police officers arrive, ready to get answers I'm not sure the girls are ready to give.

I'm wearing a trail across the hotel rug as the girls answer question after question regarding the 'accident.' First one pop, then several immediately following. My fists are aching from clenching them while listening to Julia recount the terror of that ride. When the officers appear satisfied they have enough information to launch a credible investigation, they leave their contact numbers and go on their way.

Julia insists that Tess rests in our suite, so she gets her comfortable and returns to where I'm waiting in my office. Her face is deathly white and although she tries to hide it, I see the tremble in her hands.

"Sunshine, talk to me." She sits across from me and takes a deep breath before releasing it.

"Danny paid me a visit yesterday."

"What the fuck, Julia?" I do my best to tamp down my rising anger when she holds her hands up in surrender.

"I know, I know. I was going to tell you last night, but decided to wait after I learned about your father. Then I was going to tell you this morning, but then my mother called, and things became too much. I'm sorry." My chest lurches when I take in her solemn expression. Soft lines mar her gaunt complexion. I have my own shit to deal with so I'm not exactly able to point fingers. Closing my eyes I let the irritation simmer right under the surface knowing that losing my temper won't help this situation.

I slump back against the cool leather of the armchair, steepling my fingers as I wait for her to continue. She narrows her eyes, and I know she's debating how much to share about his visit.

"Julia, whatever it is, we'll get through it together. What did Danny want?" Her laugh is maniacal.

"Well, let's see." She raises her fingers like she's ticking off a list. "First, he wants to know when I'm going to take the family business seriously. Second, he still wants to meet to discuss the takeover." Sadness washes over her beautiful face as she holds up a third finger.

"Oh, and he wants me to kill you."

Chapter

FIFTEEN

Ben

"I'm sorry, what the fuck did you just say?" My eyes are wild and my chest heaves with repressed rage.

"Well, you took that better than I thought."

I know she's trying to lighten the mood, but this clusterfuck feels like a ton of bricks raining down from a ten-story building. No matter which direction you run, you're bound to get hit by a few.

She stands and closes the distance between us, kneeling before me to take my hands in hers. Her calm demeanor is a juxtaposition to the war raging inside me. When she opens her mouth, I slide one hand from hers and silence her by pressing a finger to her lips.

"Sunshine, I'm sorry. You'll have to forgive me. It's not every day I'm told someone wants me dead." My eyes search her face and remain locked on hers as she sucks in an audible breath and turns her face away.

"God, Ben, I know. What can we do? I've reached out to my mother. I think she knows something that can help." What she's saying does little to quench this inferno raging within.

"What did Katherine say?" Her deep frown mirrors the despair that's reflected in her brown eyes. If her mother can't help us, I'll have to turn to Jackson. God knows, he has navigated his way around that family for years. I watch her walk to the drinks cabinet and pull out a bottle of Scotch and two glasses.

After pouring a healthy amount in each, she turns, offering one to me before moving to the armchair by the window. Her eyes focus on the liquid, and mine focus on her. Taking a seat across from her, I set the glass down with more force than intended. She startles at the noise, and her panicked look grabs my attention. Tears threaten the corners of her eyes, and I straighten in my seat. It doesn't take long before she breaks the silence.

"Not much. In fact, she tried to blow off my questions about my grandparents. But there's more to what she's telling me, I'm sure of it. Her silence gives me pause, but at the same time it gives me the hope I need to keep pursuing this. Especially now that the stakes are being raised."

"Do you believe her, that there's nothing to tell?" When she looks at me, I can see that she's conflicted.

"I want to believe that she wouldn't lie, but she's always been fierce in her protection of me. She just wasn't successful at protecting me from *all* the monsters under my bed." Her face pales and I don't miss the shudder that wracks her body.

I want to erase every vile act that has ever been committed against her, but even I'm not that naïve. We've both been through things that will forever live in our nightmares. Sensing her hesitation, I pull her into my arms. She feels so small and fragile, but I know my girl is anything but weak.

Lifting her chin with two fingers, I bring her gaze to mine, and I see the storm that's raging in her chocolate eyes. I move my hand to cup her cheek, and my lips graze hers in a chaste kiss. Before it can turn deeper, she pulls back.

"I need to go back to the city. Whatever information my mother has will be easier to pry out of her in a face-to-face meeting." When I give her my best 'hell no' face, she laughs, but catches herself when she sees my face is stone. "I wasn't asking permission, Ben. I need to do everything in my power to keep you safe, and if that means going back to New York and facing my mother and brother, so be it."

"I'm coming with you." Then it hits me and I'm tearing at my hair like it's on fire. "Fuck, my dad. I can't leave town until my brothers get back and we talk to our parents. Julia, promise me you'll be careful. Don't meet with Danny alone. Promise me." Her brown eyes—eyes I could drown in, shine with tears that I want to kiss away before they fall onto her beautiful cheeks. I'm not at all comfortable with what she's saying, but she is right—she doesn't need my permission to do what she believes is best to resolve this issue. She nods quickly and hides her face in my chest while I hold her close and plant soft kisses on the top of her until she pulls away. She heads into the bedroom to pack.

I'm on the phone with Knight when she comes out of the bedroom pulling a suitcase behind her. "Lucy picked Tess up just a few minutes ago. Hey man, let me call you back. We're about to head to the airport. I'll talk to you tonight." Although I didn't elaborate on the details regarding Julia's untimely return to Manhattan, I gave him enough for him to know she was going back today, alone.

Turning to face her, my eyes roam down her curvaceous body, taking in her ample breasts and the curve of her ass and how snugly her tight skirt hugs it. I let out a low growl and lick my lips, prowling toward her. "Sunshine, I don't want you to go." My breaths are ragged and shallow.

"I have to." She's biting her lower lip again, and it takes everything in me not to bite it for her. Instead, I cup her face and my lips brush hers in a kiss that quickly turns passionate. Backing her up against the door, I devour her luscious mouth. This is more than a kiss. It's urgent and intense. We're both gasping for air when she pushes at my chest, breaking our embrace.

"Easy killer. I've got a plane to catch. And you have business with your brothers. You don't want to be late." As hard as I am and as difficult as walking away is, she's right. We don't have time to start something right now.

An hour later, we've said our goodbyes and after Julia promises for the third time not to put herself in danger with Danny, I head toward the Lux. Courtland and Knight both arrived in town this afternoon. All of us will be meeting at our parents' house in about, I glance at my watch. Shit, now. I make a U-turn and after a few miles, I'm pulling up the cobblestone drive just as an unfamiliar car ahead of me slows to a stop, its brake lights flashing. I assume that's Courtland and Knight in a rental car, because Jackson's F250 rumbles into the driveway behind me. The King brothers have arrived.

Courtland and Knight exit the car as soon as the engine cuts out, and Jackson barely has his monster truck in park before he bounds out and joins us on the front lawn, giving hugs and back slaps all around. Courtland's gaze turns pensive when he considers my own expression. As much as I tried to leave out the grave details of this impromptu meeting, the summons to meet here suggests the severity of my request.

"Ben, we're here. What's this all about?" Courtland asks, his deep blue eyes darkening until they're almost black. This is something that's only noticeable to those closest to him and it only happens when he feels his control is slipping. It's a look I haven't seen since Molly was injured in the hit and run last year.

Clearing my throat, my own pain is reflected in his dark orbs. I don't want to get into this here. "Let's go inside. Mom and Dad are expecting us." Turning away before he can see my despair, I stride toward the familiar red front door.

Leading the way, my brothers can only follow. Guilt twists at my insides at how I've been unable to prepare them for what they are about to hear. It will be hard on them, on all of us, but at least I have had a little time to process the news. As usual, the door swings open before we've all made it to the porch. Our mother stands before us, always the stoic matriarch of the King family, wearing a smile that could light up the darkest night. She pulls us into a group hug. When we break apart, I don't miss the moisture gathering in her hazel eyes and I immediately fold her into another hug, this one tighter than before.

Courtland, Jackson, and Knight stand stock still while I rub circles over our petite mother's back. We both pull apart at the shuffling sound behind us. I turn to see that my dad has joined us on the porch, his eyes red rimmed and sad. When he speaks, his voice is weak, much more so than just yesterday. "Boys, you came." Spoken as if he's surprised his children are here.

"Dad, of course we're here. Let's go inside where it's warm." I try to remain casual, but when I glance at Jackson, he looks like he's lost his best friend. Knight and Courtland don't fare much better. We follow our parents into the dining room and take seats around the rustic farm table as our mom slides into a chair, her focus remaining on our dad, never wavering.

"Boys, please forgive me. Your dad and I have practiced this meeting so many times, I thought I could get through this with dry eyes."

Knight moves to stand behind Mom, his steady hands holding her shoulders as he leans forward to brush his cheek against hers.

"Mom, don't be sorry. We're here. Whatever it is, we can handle it." I'm not sure who he is trying harder to convince—her, my dad, or my brothers and me. Before she can get the next words out, I decide to help lighten this burden.

"Mom, let me." Her eyes flash to mine and her tears begin to fall anew. I've never felt so helpless. Not even when I was caught up in the Baldoni shit after the car accident, or even when Julia was taken earlier this year. Those were unthinkable situations, but this is on a whole different spectrum.

Our parents, our rock, are crumbling at our feet like stones eroded by years of being battled by the ocean's current. I know what comes next, and I am determined to spare her and Dad the torture of having to say it aloud. Knight returns to his seat and the six of us link hands around the table, joined in solidarity. I take a deep breath and address my brothers.

"Mom and Dad gave me some unexpected news regarding Dad's health just before I contacted each of you about this meeting."

The next two hours are excruciating. I relay our mother's words, the doctor's detailed prognosis and the missed diagnosis revolving around Dad's treatment. That he is no longer in remission, and they have exhausted all treatment options. The doctors estimate we have three to six months left to enjoy him. I watch painfully as my brothers' expressions change from bewilderment, to shock, and finally to unbelievable acquiescence.

We share a few more tears and hugs and promise to meet tomorrow. As we each pull away from the house, I am consumed with dread. Checking my phone, I see the text I've been waiting for and am flooded with relief.

> Julia: Made it back in one piece. Meeting with Mom tomorrow morning at ten.

My fingers fly across the keys as I shoot a reply.

Me: Glad to hear. Hide all sharp objects. My meeting went as well as could be expected. Talk to you soon.

DAY SURRENDERS TO night as I drive toward the hotel. Streetlights appear in the distance while the last shades of purple and pink fade to black. Pulling into my parking spot, I dial Jackson's number. I didn't intend for tonight to be about anything other than our dad, but now that that conversation is over, I need to focus on the next big thing. Anger and frustration have been brewing just below the surface for a while now. As soon as Jackson picks up, my words are as cold as the night air and I shock even myself.

"It's time. How do we take down the Baldonis?"

Chapter SIXTEEN

Julia

When my eyes focus, I see it's six in the morning. I toss and turn for two hours before I drag myself out of bed and make my way to the bathroom. It only takes a few minutes for the water to warm to the perfect temperature. Stepping under the showerhead, I close my eyes, lean my head against the slate tile, and allow the cool surface and the heated water droplets to ground me. Reaching for the body wash, I pour a small amount onto my sponge and quickly scrub myself clean before shampooing my hair. I turn off the shower and grab two fluffy white towels, wrapping my hair in one while tucking the other around my body.

I need to be on my game today when I meet my mom. Heading into the walk-in closet, my eyes land on a pair of black skinny jeans and an off-the-shoulder cream cashmere sweater. After toweling my hair dry, I pull it into a high pony and dress, choosing tall flat boots to complete my look. Not wanting to overdo my makeup, I apply a blush, bronzer, and mascara and then pull up the app to order a ride.

As I wait for the driver, guilt pricks my insides. I didn't tell Ben the complete plan for today. He knows I'm meeting my mother, but I conveniently left out the part where I was going to meet Danny and Joey later this afternoon. Knowing he would go ballistic and probably catch the next flight to New York, I couldn't risk it. He needs to be with his family, and I've taken enough time away from them. Tonight, I'll tell him about both meetings.

I'm checking my texts when a dark sedan rolls up to the building entrance. I open the door and slide in without checking to see if it's the car I requested. As soon as the door closes, the sound of locks clicking punctures the air. Noticing the driver peering at me from his side of the partition, I give a nervous chuckle and murmur something about keeping his patrons safe and shit. He doesn't answer but shifts his eyes ahead as he pulls into traffic. Something about the driver rings familiar and I try to place where I've seen him before. Curiosity gets the best of me when my mental search comes up empty. Clearing my throat, I meet his gaze in the mirror.

"Excuse me, but have we met before?" My words come out breathy, which certainly wasn't planned. He cocks a dark brow but doesn't immediately speak. I squirm in the leather seat feeling awkward as fuck until he finally breaks the tense silence.

"Miller, ma'am." His voice is soft, just above a whisper, and I have to strain to catch his words.

"You work for my mother." It's a statement instead of a question. He nods slightly and returns his gaze to the road. I pull up the app to cancel my ride request, then relax into the buttery soft leather. I close my eyes against the harsh light and drift off. When I open my eyes, the car is parked outside my mother's Fifth Avenue apartment building. Miller sits behind the wheel, a subtle smile tilting his lips as he glances over his shoulder where I'm slumped into the seat in a post-nap haze.

"You're awake." Not sure how long we've been parked, I shake myself and turn to open the door, but he indicates for me to wait. He gets out and rounds the front of the car, clutches the handle and opens my door. I give a subtle nod in his direction along with a tight smile as I step onto the sidewalk. A sense of dread coats my mind. My mother hasn't always been the easiest woman to talk to. I've never doubted her fierce love for me, but sometimes it feels like she's keeping me at arm's length, especially when it relates to business matters. That's why I'm not particularly optimistic about how this conversation will go. How forthcoming she will be when it comes to her side of the family remains to be seen.

I walk past the security desk, noting the absence of the usual officer. Stepping into the elevator, I press the button that will deliver me directly to the penthouse. Katherine Tolliver has always thrived in the lap of luxury. Even as a little girl, before my life imploded, I remember having servants at our disposal, although I thought they were just helpers who lived with us. It wasn't until my father came into the picture that I learned they were actually hired staff who worked for my mother. I grew particularly close to a couple of the older women, as they seemed to fulfill a grandmotherly role in my life.

I'm lost in my memories when the elevator doors slide open and my eyes land on my mother standing before me. She is a picture of elegance even at this early hour. Squaring my shoulders, I step into the living room and greet her with a warm hug. I pull away first and she motions me to follow her into the kitchen.

"Julia, I'm glad you made it back. I gave Cook the day off, so I'll get our coffee. Shall we?" I try to hide the shock that plays across my face at her statement. I didn't even know she knew how to make coffee.

Settling myself at the granite bar top, I lean forward on my elbows while she prepares two mugs and slides one in front of me. I carefully wrap my hands around the hot mug and meet her gaze. Releasing a deep sigh, she narrows her eyes and dips her head slightly. "So, I guess you're here for answers?" Her voice is quiet as she takes a seat across from me. She opened the door, so I might as well step in.

"Yes, Mom. I'm here for answers. Danny threatened Ben, and I need to find a way to beat him at his own game. Is there anything you can tell me about my grandparents that might help me in gaining the upper hand?" I blink at her several times while I wait for a response. Anything I can add to my arsenal and use against the Baldonis. She opens her mouth, closes it again and her face goes pale. I catch the shift in her eyes before she hides it away.

"Oh, Sweetheart, why do you think my parents have anything to do with that family? They both died before you were even born. They barely knew the Baldonis." There's something about her posture that causes doubt to creep in. She is lying and I can't figure out why. After all this time, why keep secrets? I won't push it for now, so I finish my coffee and stand to leave. This was a wasted morning, but I remember that she wanted to talk to me when I came home.

"Mom, you mentioned you wanted to talk to me when I came back. Does this have anything to do with Michael? It's been twelve years since I ran away, but now that the family is trying to force me in, I'm afraid I haven't heard the last of him." The words are like acid on my tongue. Her eyes widen for a split second, then she recovers and flashes me a small smile.

"Oh, no Honey. I told you not to worry about Michael. We can talk later. I know you have that meeting. You don't want to be late." I pause—I never told her what time I was meeting Danny. There's something more going on where she's concerned, but I'm not going to push it. At least not yet. Giving her a kiss on the cheek, I leave.

I'm still pondering this in the elevator. The same dark sedan is parked in front of the building. The driver stands, holding the door open, but I notice it isn't Miller. Without a word, I slide into the back seat and suddenly it becomes apparent I'm not alone. Before I can question the intruder, I feel a sharp prick on my neck. My eyes land on the passenger. "Son of a bitch." Before I finish the protest, my world fades to darkness.

MY EYES FLUTTER as I endeavor to open them, the banging sensation of a sledgehammer to the brain making me groan. *Shit, what happened to me?* My first instinct is to fight against whatever holds me, and every muscle in my body is screaming for relief. My futile attempts to move are thwarted by the restraints holding my arms in place.

"What the fuck…" My voice trails off as my eyes crack open slightly to reveal my brother standing in front of me. It takes several tries before I'm able to focus and my head lolls forward as a wave of nausea crests and acid rises in my throat.

"Good, you're awake." Even in my drugged-up state, I recognize the voice of the devil. It takes an enormous amount of energy, but I lift my head and meet his evil gaze.

"Danny, what the fuck?" My words are slurred, and for a minute I don't think he's going to answer me. Determined to hold his stare, I focus on keeping my eyelids open and wait him out. He finally cocks his head to the side and a demonic smirk crosses his mouth.

"Is that any kind of greeting for your brother? I don't think you're in any position to bite, Julia Bear."

My vision clears a little more; I turn my head slightly and see that we're in my father's old office. Whenever I was summoned here as a child, I left in tears. I vow that this time will be different.

I catch movement to my side and Joey comes into view. He's across the room opposite where Danny stands. He's the youngest son so his word carries shit, but right now I need to explore my options. That's why I slide my gaze to him.

"Joey, what the hell is going on? Did you drug me?" They must have, that must have been the pinprick I felt when I got into the car outside my mother's apartment. Though my speech is still slow, Joey must hear resolve in my voice, because I don't have to wait long for him to answer. Of all my brothers, Joey is the one you can reason with. Not like Brando or Danny, who change the rules to suit whatever bullshit they are doing.

"Julia, believe me, this wasn't my idea." I do believe him. That's the problem. Danny is a lone wolf who acts first and asks questions later. He turns his attention to our brother. "Danny you got her here — now untie her." When he makes no move to loosen my restraints, Joey speaks again. This time there's irritation in his voice. "Either you untie her, or I will."

Once again Danny remains where he stands, lording over my small frame. "Oh for fuck's sake." Joey gives an exasperated sigh and runs a hand through his dark hair before moving to where they've sat me and bending to remove the ropes from my wrists and ankles. Ignoring Danny, I focus my attention on Joey as I rub my wrists, trying to get the feeling back.

"Thank you." Twisting my body around to level a glare at Danny, I'm suddenly filled with contempt at my brother's behavior. The drug-fueled haze has almost cleared, giving way to a state of cognizance — and defiance.

"You can just stop with the theatrics, Daniel. You made your point, although you knew I was coming this afternoon anyway, so what gives? Why pull the drugging act? That's a new low even for you." I can't stop myself from uttering words I'd been holding on to for so long. It's like a dam has burst and the flood gates can't hold back the impending destruction any longer. I give him everything I have. "You know, I should have killed you long ago." My eyes are blazing as I focus on his smug face, ready to punch it if he so much as breathes the wrong way.

"As if you could, big sis." He doesn't hide the amusement he finds in my words, just gives a chuckle. But when his eyes find mine again, all traces of humor are long erased and in its place is the cold, calculating son of a bitch who lives to make my life a misery. That was what he tried to do while we were under the same roof, but that was years ago. I'm not that helpless little girl anymore, although I'm still trying to heal from the emotional scars he inflicted on me.

As much as I despise him and as strong as I've become, there's still a small part of me that's terrified of him and the evil he's capable of. I'm not particularly afraid for my safety, but Ben must be protected at all costs.

After I get the feeling back in my hands and feet, I'm a little steadier, and I stand and make my way over to the drinks cabinet and pour myself a glass of water. Whatever drug is in my system, it's making me thirsty as hell. Raising the glass to my lips, I drain it in one gulp. I'm just about to refute his words when he laughs again, and my eyes focus on something in his hand. It's a phone. My phone.

"Oh, my bad. You might want to respond to all these missed calls and texts. Let me guess, Loverboy doesn't know we are having a family meeting today? That disappoints me, Julia. To think you can't be honest with the guy you're fucking. What does that say about your relationship and the level of trust you apparently don't have with him? Tell me, what will he say when he finds out about your husband?" He tsks and cold chills run down my spine. I've never wanted to murder anyone like I want to murder my half-brother at this moment. I truly believe I could squeeze the life out of him using only my bare hands.

For some reason I can't quite explain, I take several deep breaths before snatching my phone out of his hands and turning my attention to Joey. At least he will listen to reason when he doesn't feel threatened. That's how I remember him when our shit would go sideways. I can't necessarily say I trust him, but it's more than I can say for my other brother.

"Joey, can you talk some sense into your evil twin?" I can't even look at Danny for fear I might grab the first sharp object I can find and stab his eyeballs out. When I meet Joey's gaze, he just shrugs matter-of-factly and turns his attention to the devil in front of us. I'm standing, arms crossed over my chest and waiting for whatever comes next. I don't have to wait long as Danny straightens his back and gives a deep sigh. For a fleeting moment something passes over his expression but as fast as it crosses his face, it is gone, again. Before I can question him, he speaks.

"Look, I'm just following protocol according to our father's will." What the fuck? Now I'm regretting sitting that reading out, but Jackson had attended, and he never mentioned anything about murder—then again, that would have been a top secret clause that the parties attending would not have been privy to. While these thoughts run through my mind, Danny's standing there smug as fuck, picking an imaginary piece of lint from his jacket. I huff in frustration.

"What the hell, Danny? Protocol? You wouldn't know protocol if it jumped up and bit you in the ass." Joey snorts at the visual I'd just given him and Danny scowls in return.

"All I'm saying, Julia Bear, is that Carmine Baldoni stated in his will that retribution was owed for Leah's death five years ago and that the punishment for this long overlooked crime is death."

"Crime?" I can't believe what I'm hearing. "Jesus, Danny, it was a tragic accident. One which our family had a hand in both framing Ben and covering it up—you said as much two days ago. Don't you think the Baldonis should receive some of this so-called retribution?"

"So, what do you propose, dear sister?" There was that mocking tone that I wanted to slap right off his motherfucking face, but I know if I want to make any progress with him, I need to remain calm and pray he'll decide enough blood has been spilled to last several lifetimes. Yeah, when pigs fly. Danny has always been full of blood lust, even more than Brando, and I bet this situation gives him a hard on just talking about it. Propping my hands on my hips, I stand dumbfounded as both guys stare back at me—Joey with curiosity and Danny with daggers in his eyes.

"What if I refuse? As head of the family, I can veto this ridiculous notion and never speak of it again." As much as I want to believe my own words, I know I don't hold that kind of power, even in my unwanted position. Carmine Baldoni squashed any option that would negate his authority.

There must be a way around this. "Isn't it time to stop the bloodshed? Can't we move past this and coexist in mutual concordance?" Danny continues to look at me like I've grown two heads while Joey snickers to himself. "What? Is that such an egregious request?"

"Julia, you're a bright woman, surely you can figure it out. But just in case, let me spell it out for you. Your guy's days are numbered and there's no way out of it." Danny's eyes twinkle and I'm one hundred percent certain he's turned on by the degree of violence those words hold. Raising his hands in surrender, he continues. "Hey, I get it. If all the starry eyes and romantic shit has you second guessing your ability, I'll be more than happy to step in and take one for the team."

I can't help myself. One minute I'm standing practically nose to nose with my brother, then in a flash my hand flies to his face and the crack of my slap rings out around me. The hit lands hard enough that his head whips to the side. I turn and head out the door.

There must be another way. If I must burn the entire city down to save the man I love, then so be it. Even if it means I'm burnt in the process, I'll do it. Cradling my hand, I make my way out to the street as my phone rings. Rolling my eyes and stifling a groan, I press the answer button, but as soon as the call connects, I'm met with an angry growl from the sexiest man I know. Under any other circumstance I would consider it foreplay, but something tells me this isn't about sexy anything.

"Sunshine, where the fuck are you?"

Whoopsie!

Julia

"Hey Ben, I can explain." I can't hear anything on the other end except heavy breaths. God, is he panting?

"Damn right. Now start explaining." I open my mouth to speak but he just unloads on me, and I let him. I guess I deserve it after fourteen unanswered texts and eight missed calls. "Dammit it, Julia. Didn't I tell you not to meet with that bastard brother of yours? What were you thinking?" The strained words fly from his mouth, like if he doesn't get them out now, he'll never get another chance.

As soon as he takes a breath, I find my opportunity. "Ben, I thought I could get some information out of him, but he's still adamant Carmine's wishes must be fulfilled. And how do you know I was with him? Are you having me followed?"

"What? No. Fuck. Maybe I should if you're going to insist on remaining reckless where that jackass is concerned, but no, when you didn't answer my calls or texts, I put two and two together. You're damn lucky you answered because I was about to hop on Courtland's private jet and head back to New York."

"Dramatic much?" I can't help myself. I know he's worried, but come on. "Look, I'm sorry, but if I'm being honest, I was drugged and kidnapped." The line goes silent, too silent. I hear a sharp intake of air and a slow exhale.

"What the fuck did you say? I'll kill him."

"Take a number. He was just wielding his big dick energy." I try to make my voice light and nonchalant, but he can see right through that tactic.

"Uh-huh, not this time. I almost lost you once. I won't let you take those kinds of risks again." There's no arguing with him about this. He's right, neither of my brothers can be trusted and things seem to be escalating faster than I first thought. I hear the anxiety coming through in his voice and I'm suddenly consumed with guilt for keeping him in the dark.

"I'm sorry, Ben. It's just frustrating not being in control and not getting a good read on my brother's misguided loyalty to a dead man, even if he was our father." I hear his deep exhale over the phone again.

"Sunshine, please don't apologize. I know you're frustrated and afraid of what Danny might do, but we can't live in fear. Look, Knight is due back in town tomorrow. As soon as he arrives, I'll fly back. In the meantime, I just spoke to Courtland and Molly is expecting a girl's night tonight." His tone turns playful.

"You couldn't have led with that?" I can't help the smile that tugs at my mouth. He chuckles and I continue. "Thank you, Ben." As the words leave my mouth, the familiar beep of an incoming call sounds in my ear. "Oh, hey this is Molly now. Talk to you later?"

"You bet, and Sunshine? I'm calling in extra security around your apartment. Try to relax and have some fun tonight." I just smile as I cut the call, switching to where my friend is waiting.

"Molly, hey. It's good to hear from you." I wasn't lying. Molly is the type of friend who, despite a childhood tragedy, always sees the glass half full and she will do anything to make sure others are well cared for. Before I even hear her voice, my mood is starting to improve.

"Hey, Julia, back at you. So tonight, dinner and drinks? How about it? Courtland just got back this morning. We can kick him out and have the apartment to ourselves, or we can go out. Name your poison?" Her gentle laughter soothes the ache forming in my stomach while I turn the options over in my mind. I don't want to make Courtland leave considering he's just returned from Stone Creek, but would the extra security Ben arranged carry over to a restaurant or club?

I am about to ask if she wants to order take-out and come my way, when she takes the decision out of my hands, and I'm thankful for the gesture. "Look, I know things are tense with your family right now." That was a hell of an understatement—if she only knew. "How about this? Courtland and I can pick you up around eight. We'll go to a nice restaurant, banish him to a corner where he can keep watch from a distance, and you and I can enjoy the evening with a semblance of privacy. What do you think?"

That sounds like an offer I can't refuse except for one caveat. "Anywhere except Black Diamond Club." My voice is shaky as the words fall from my mouth.

"Oh honey, if I never step foot in that place again, it will be too soon." Yeah, Black Diamond Club, Brando's club, was where Lucy and I were drugged and kidnapped earlier this year. Apparently, Danny has taken over now. No way would I be caught dead in there. In fact, dead would be the only way I'd be there.

After a few beats of awkward silence, she continues. "Okay, it's settled then. We'll pick you up at eight and blow the top off this town.

I'd say we're overdue, wouldn't you?" The only thing I am interested in blowing the top off of at this moment is Danny's head, but that will have to wait. Tonight is about reconnecting with friends and forgetting this shit show, if only just for a little while. So instead of mentioning my penchant for violence toward my younger brother, I grit my teeth and say what she's waiting to hear. "Sure, Molly. It'll be great. See you at eight."

AFTER LOCKING MY door and making my way down the steps, I reach the sidewalk just as a black limo rounds the corner, coming to a stop at my feet. I recognize Courtland's driver immediately and when he opens the door, I slide into the softest buttery Italian leather seats ever. Seriously, these seats can rival my own memory foam mattress in the softness department.

I groan not so quietly, which makes Molly laugh as Courtland just shakes his head with a smile on his face. Yeah, these seats have served a higher purpose, if the blush that's apparent on my friend's face is any indication.

I buckle in after Molly squeals and pulls me into a tight embrace, then we are on our way. "Where are we going?" Molly shoots Courtland a look and he just shrugs. So apparently I'll have to wait. It doesn't matter what our destination is as long as I'm with my friend. I'm ready to let loose and have some harmless fun.

We are only a couple blocks down the road when I start second guessing my wardrobe choice. As soft as the seats are, my ass is freezing against the cool leather where my short dress has begun to ride up my thighs. I can't blame anyone but myself for not choosing more appropriate evening attire, especially since Ben isn't here to fully appreciate my efforts. We make light conversation as the car winds through several intersections before rolling up to a black granite building. I recognize this building although I have never been here.

Smoke and Mirrors is an upscale restaurant and bar that vets its patrons like they are entering the White House or something. We're essentially body scanned as we walk through metal detectors before being led to a table in the back corner of the restaurant. My eyes dart around to find the room essentially empty. Courtland places a chaste kiss to Molly's lips before turning toward a table close enough in case we need anything, but far enough to give us the privacy we crave.

My mouth falls open as it dawns on me that Courtland must have reserved this place especially for the three of us. I just stare at Molly as she casually picks up the menu, unfazed by our surroundings. Clearing my throat, I force out a laugh.

"Molly, did Courtland rent out the entire restaurant?" Her eyes widen as she realizes for the first time that, except for the three of us, the room is empty. That's exactly what her husband has done, and I could kiss him. Who knew the ruthless King brother could be so thoughtful.

"Huh, I guess he did." Her response holds little surprise. That was Courtland King, ever the thoughtful husband. We're both huddled over our menus when the waiter appears beside our table. I guess we will have his undivided attention tonight seeing as there are no other customers present.

"Ladies, welcome to Smoke and Mirrors. The sommelier will be with you shortly." As he turns to walk away, I call out. "Sir, I think I'd like to order a cocktail if you don't mind." He smiles politely and within minutes we are nursing the citrusy flavor of one of the best Cosmos that has ever touched my lips. Heaven in a glass.

"So, Julia, it's been a hot minute since we've talked. What's going on with your family?" I can't help the grimace that pulls at my mouth. I know it's inevitable that this topic comes up. After all, it's not every day you find out you're the head of one of the most dangerous crime families in the country, even if it is by default.

Picking up my glass, I down the remainder and when my eyes meet our waiter, I lift my glass for another. "How much time do we have?" I chuckle, but there isn't any humor behind the sound. When I give an exasperated sigh, my friend takes my hand in hers.

"Oh Jules, is it that bad?" She's blinking her eyes, waiting for whatever I might hit her with. Blowing out a breath, I turn my full attention to her.

"It's worse." Her eyes begin to tear up as she squeezes my hand harder. "It's okay though, I'm working on a plan to cut ties with the family permanently." I'm not sure where that came from. There is no plan, only wishful thinking that someone will eliminate Danny, and I'll be free to continue living my life as I want, without looking over my shoulder for the rest of it. Molly nods in agreement and we motion the waiter to take our food orders before we get stoned drunk.

After ordering another drink and devouring the biggest steak on the Eastern seaboard, we push away from the table, both of us on the verge of a food coma. I've filled her in on Danny's asinine behavior and we're about to join Courtland at his table when my phone rings. My first instinct is to ignore it, but when I see it's my mother calling, something makes me hit green instead of red.

"Hello, Mother." My tone is sharp, but she doesn't respond to my greeting. After a few failed attempts to get her attention, I figure out she air-dialed me and doesn't know I connected the call. Before I give up and end the call, I realize she's speaking to someone— oblivious to my accidental intrusion. Part of me feels guilty for continuing to listen, but the other part is curious to see how much she'll spill before she realizes her mistake.

Pressing a finger to my mouth, I hit the speaker and prop the phone up in front of me. It becomes quickly obvious that she is drunk.

That's odd. I've never known her to have more than a couple of drinks and even then, her speech is never affected. As I continue my privacy breach, it's apparent the other person, a man, is agitated, the volume of his voice getting louder until I finally hear my mother's voice again.

"Look Marco, I need those records. It's important." My eyes widen as I try to make sense of what she's saying. The only Marco I know is one of my father's corporate attorneys, but why would she be talking to him? Raised voices permeate the air before the line goes dead. *Shit.*

"What the fuck?" While I focused on the conversation between my mother and my father's lawyer, Courtland joined us. His gaze is suspicious as I run my hand across my face and blow out a big breath.

"What was that about?" I sit blinking at my friend.

"The hell if I know." The call cut off before I could get enough information, but one thing is certain. I'll be paying Katherine Tolliver another visit tomorrow morning. Shaking my head, I drain the last of my drink.

"I'm sorry ladies, but I need to stop by the office and pick up some documents. You can come with me, or I can have the driver come back for you when I'm done." He is trying to be supportive, but his face tells a different story. He's worried about the conversation I stumbled onto. Not wanting to be any more trouble than I already feel I've been, I tell Molly I need to get back, anyway. I had promised to call Ben when I got home, and I intend to make good use of the miles which separate us.

It is just after ten-thirty when the car pulls up to my building. I hold a hand up when Courtland shifts to open his door. "It's okay. I think I can manage the short walk to my building. You don't need to get out." When he realizes I'm not going to budge, Molly says they will wait for me to get through my door before pulling away. I release an exaggerated sigh but smile and pull her into a hug before sliding out the door and into the crisp night air.

After unlocking the door, I pause, sending a wave to my friends and then close the door quickly, careful to lock it and set the alarm before padding into the kitchen to find a glass of water.

The lingering effects of whatever drug Danny shot into my system are still kicking my butt. Maybe it wasn't such a smart idea to have those drinks tonight. Sitting at the bar, staring into the empty water glass, I replay the night's events. Recalling some of the truths I shared with Molly about my family and my mother's strange conversation leaves my nerves frazzled.

After a few minutes, I trudge to my bedroom, peel off my dress and kick off my shoes. Wearing only panties and a bra, I make my way toward the bathroom. A quick shower and sleep are what I really need. Except for a nice dinner with my best friend, I'm ready to put this day to bed.

Rest up Mother dear. Tomorrow, you owe me answers and I intend to collect in spades.

Chapter
EIGHTEEN

Ben

I'm practically grinding my teeth by the time Julia ends the call—especially after what she said she heard when her mother air-dialed her. At least she remembered to call me when she returned from her night out with Molly. Jackson hasn't offered much in the way of eliminating Danny from the equation, aside from straight up murder, and as appealing as the idea sounds, I'd like to handle this with minimal violence.

I'm still sitting at the Lux bar when a bottle is placed in front of me, followed by an empty glass, and I look over to see Jackson with a smug look on his face. For some reason, that look sets my temper off.

"Oh fuck off, Jack. What are you even doing here?" I hate taking out my aggressions on others, but he makes a damn easy target. I'm glaring at my brother as he raises his hands.

"Look, man. I know you're having a hard time with your girl gone and all, but don't piss on me just because you can't deal." The look of determination on his face makes me scowl. Even though Courtland and I are older, Jackson has never had a problem putting us in our place if we deserve it, and at this moment I sure as shit deserve to be called out for my outburst.

"You're right. I'm sorry, I'm just having a hard time dealing with this bullshit the Baldonis are trying to pull with Julia and she's playing right into it taking chances where she shouldn't be." I rake my hand through my hair and pour the Macallan to the rim of the glass. Taking it in my hand, I down it and immediately pour another. Jackson remains silent at my side.

"I should just hire a hit and end this for good." As soon as the words leave my mouth, I'm shaking my head. Robert and Olivia King didn't raise killers, aside from the fact I shot Brando Baldoni, but that was self-defense. In our family, there's always another way to solve problems without resorting to violence. But sadly, we aren't talking about the King family. It's the fucked-up family that Julia was cursed with that needs to be dealt with.

My brother, sensing the heaviness of the night, seems to try to lighten the conversation. "I bet Courtland knows a guy. You don't get to his level of success without having some hired muscle in your pocket."

That statement takes me by surprise, and I grimace. "Are you saying Courtland has the means to order a hit?" Surely that's not what my brother is implying.

Jackson just chuckles while shaking his head. "Relax, Ben. I'm just saying maybe we should rally the troops like we did with the Brando situation. Let them know who really calls the shots." I don't disagree, but the last time the four of us took on the Baldoni fucks, our girls damn near got killed. At least that's how I remember that awful day.

After we finish off the bottle of Scotch, Jackson stands, pulling me into a man hug and we both call it a night. Exhaustion pulls at every muscle as if I had engaged in some type of MMA fight, but that's what stress can do to the body, and I am fucking stressed. I won't fully relax until I hold Julia in my arms. After telling Jack goodnight, I make my way to my suite.

Stepping into the shower, my mind immediately goes to the petite brunette with chocolate eyes. The one who owns my heart as well as my dick. I stand under the multi-jet faucet as the water pummels my back and courses down my body. Grabbing my aching cock, I give it a couple of hard pulls and my head drops back against the marble tile while visions of a goddess play out in front of me.

With closed eyes, I let my imagination have its way with me. My hand begins to move faster to an invisible beat and low groans slip past my lips. I feel my orgasm building, and it won't be long before my release creates a kaleidoscope of sensations that takes me beyond the edge of ecstasy.

As if on cue, my body jerks and hot cum covers the tile in front of me. The sensation seems to go on forever until my body convulses from the aftershocks, leaving me in a boneless heap against the shower wall. Catching my breath and adjusting the spray, I take time to clean the wall before I turn off the water. I grab a bath towel, wrapping it loosely around my waist and make my way to the dresser. After drying off, I pull on a pair of gray sweats and a black t-shirt.

I take a beer from the mini-fridge and fall back on the bed, propping myself up with the myriad of pillows housekeeping refreshed this morning. My eyes drift to the bedside clock and I note it's just before midnight. My body buzzes with nervous energy, and I can't unwind enough to keep my eyes closed. Neither the Macallan nor the beer is enough to dull the worries plaguing my brain. Anxiety courses through my veins like amphetamine, imposing a high on my body.

I'm not certain how long I toss and turn before my phone rings. A groan escapes my mouth as a familiar name flashes in the darkness. I press to connect the call to video.

"You have that twin thing going on again?" It's a couple beats before my brother's eyes narrow and his voice breaks the silence.

"What? Uh, no. You really believe that bullshit? It's nothing like that. Jackson called earlier and he was proposing some pretty fucked up shit." Of course, Jackson had called Courtland. Why wasn't I surprised? Before he can tell me what I already know, I interrupt him.

"Look, Jackson has a twisted way of looking at this. Whatever he said and whatever spin he put on it, let's just forget it." I scrape my hand through my hair and blow out a long exhale. I can tell he's assessing the situation, though, when he cocks his head to the side and gives a lopsided grin.

"You're awfully chipper for it to be the middle of the night. You get laid or something?" My tone holds humor, but there is something playful about my brother's expression.

"Or something," he deadpans. Rolling my eyes, I level a glare at him.

"This is serious, man. Julia believes her mother may hold the key to ending this clusterfuck, but she's not talking."

"You need someone to lean on her. I know a guy who owes me a favor." His words come through as if I'd asked for a lawn service recommendation.

"Fuck, no. That won't be necessary. Jesus, Courtland, does everything come down to power and violence with you?" I don't think my twin is capable of that level of brutality, but when push comes to shove and all that shit… He just shrugs and then his expression turns serious.

"No, man, but when family is involved, power and violence are in the eye of the beholder. Julia is family to you and by extension she belongs to the rest of us. If her family really is as threatening as you think they are, we need to expedite a strategy to bring them to their knees

He isn't wrong, but even I know wishing something into reality isn't always a possibility. That's why I give a subtle head shake at his words.

"You're right about one thing, brother. We need to plan a strategic strike they will never see coming, one that will minimize collateral damage the most."

Scrubbing a hand over my face, I can't believe what I'm about to say. "Okay, I'll be back in Manhattan tomorrow afternoon. Let's meet and compare notes to see how we can bring these motherfuckers down for good. Let's see if your guy is as good as you say." I was goading him on, but I didn't really care at this point. If Danny had stooped to the low of drugging his own sister, there's probably not much he wouldn't do to secure his place at the helm of power in the city.

Courtland just flips me off as I end the call. Bastard. I laugh to myself. It's well after one, so I settle back onto the bed and this time when I close my eyes, visions of blood and violence dance through my head, bringing with it one of the best night's sleep I've had in a long time.

Danny Baldoni has another thing coming if he thinks I'll just play nice while he puts a bullet in my head. Get ready, motherfucker, the Kings are coming for you.

Chapter
NINETEEN

Julia

I startle awake at the sound of a door closing. Immediately my heart is in my throat and my eyes scan the dark room for wherever the unwelcome sound came from. Sliding from the bed, I try to not rustle the sheets as I grab my robe from the hook and shrug it on over my sleep shirt and underwear. I tie my robe around my waist and then tiptoe to my nightstand and lift the Glock from its resting place. Even having grown up with an arsenal at my fingertips, guns still make me jumpy.

My heart races and I can feel sweat on the back of my neck as I stumble to my bedroom door. Hmm. The door is closed, but I don't remember closing it last night. Sucking in a deep breath, then twisting the knob, I release the breath as the door swings open. "Hello." When I'm met with only silence, I begin creeping down the hall. After checking every room, I'm still confused as to the sound that woke me.

I make my way into the kitchen. It's early, but there's no point in going back to bed, so I head to the coffee maker—and remember that I'm out of coffee. A string of curses falls from my mouth. I hastily dress and walk to the corner cafe.

I spend the next two hours indulging in a self-induced caffeine high. To balance the caffeine, I polish off the day's special of three pancakes, stacked high and oozing with syrup and butter, along with bacon and eggs. The antique grandfather clock in the corner chimes and it's seven o'clock, late enough for both Ben and my mother to be awake. I pick up my phone and tap the number for Ben's phone. He answers on the third ring.

"Sunshine, hey, I'm sorry. I didn't have my phone on me. What are you doing up this early?" I laugh at his question because he makes it sound as if I have a habit of sleeping late. I just roll my eyes.

"Very funny, sir. I wanted to let you know I'm headed to see my mother again this morning. After what happened last night, I'm more convinced than ever that she's withholding information that is vital to bringing down the Baldonis." Ben doesn't respond right away, which makes me pause. "What are you thinking? What did Courtland say when you talked to him?" I'm about to lose it over the phone while I wait for his reply.

"We didn't talk at length, I just gave him the highlights. Apparently, Jackson had already informed him of the situation and he was preparing to stage a coup, going in with guns blazing." I hear the apprehension in his voice, which gives me an unsettled feeling.

"Does he know who he's dealing with? My brother isn't afraid of empty threats and I'm sure he is doubling down on his security as we speak." God, I hope I'm wrong, but I can't see any of the Baldonis quietly walking away from a vow, and according to the family that's exactly what a request from the grave is.

"Sunshine, I know you're worried, but trust me. We'll be fine. As soon as Knight gets back, I'm on the next flight out. Courtland agreed that we'd meet to discuss next steps then." His words do little to calm my frayed nerves, but until I speak to my mother, we're all still in danger from whatever lurks on the horizon.

As soon as we end the call, I tap the number to my mother's phone. When her sunny voice comes over the line, she sounds like she's been up for hours, despite how slurred I remember her speech being on the unintended call to me last night. In fact, she sounds better than I've heard her in a while.

"Darling, what a surprise. Is everything alright?" My mouth falls open. In all my adult years of talking to Katherine Tolliver, she has never asked if I was alright. Something definitely is up, and I intend to find out what as soon as I can get there.

I cautiously choose my next words. "Good morning, Mom. I'm fine. Just wondering if you are going to be home this morning. I'd like to stop by if that's okay." There is a definite pause on her end before she responds in a clipped tone.

"Oh, yes of course dear. I'll have Cook serve brunch. Is eleven good for you?" Yeah, this isn't a social call although I don't tell her that. I think the element of surprise will better suit this conversation.

"Sure. I'll see you then." I keep my answer to the point. If I elaborate on the reason for my visit, I'll give too much away. I'm already on a slippery slope when it comes to how tight lipped she can be when the situation suits her.

When I hang up, I notice it's only eight thirty. I have time to stop by the studio before heading out to my mother's place. Since it's a warm day, I decide to walk the six blocks to the studio. After my experience yesterday, I don't want to take a chance on another incident with Danny. It's Sunday, which means there are no classes today, so I am able to get some paperwork done while I wait for brunch.

At exactly ten thirty, my alarm goes off. I tend to lose track of time when I'm working, so I always set the timer to avoid missing meetings, and this visit to my mother is no different. I'm tired of fucking around. Today I'll get answers.

The clouds have cleared and the Uber drops me off a couple minutes shy of eleven. I'm greeted by a new security guard, a middle-aged man I don't recognize. "Good morning. I'm here to see Ms. Tolliver. I'm her daughter, Julia." I'm getting more weirded out by the second as the man's gaze travels down my body and back up, lingering a little too long on my breasts. I cross my arms over my chest and raise my chin in defiance. When he finally meets my eyes, there's a dark expression on his face and a callous smile on his lips.

"I'm Edward. Let me see if your mother is available." He narrows his eyes as he speaks. It's almost like he doesn't believe I'm her daughter. Whatever, asshole, go ahead and make the call. I can't wait for my mother to tear you a new one.

I tap my nails on the desk while he picks up the phone and makes the call. When he announces my presence, there's a long pause. His face reddens as he listens to whoever is on the line—my mother, I assume. After a few more awkward moments, he hangs up and glares at me, his piercing blue eyes shooting daggers my way. Whatever was said on the phone didn't make him happy, that I'm certain of.

He doesn't speak again, just points behind me to the bank of elevators. The glass doors on the end cab slide open and I walk in and push the button for the penthouse. I am ready to leave Grumpy and his assholery below.

When the doors open again, I step into the penthouse, but I don't see anyone right away. I've been here countless times, and the elegance of this space never gets old. I'm happy my mother has found her contentment. It only took three failed marriages before she decided she didn't need a man to feel fulfilled.

Walking into the formal living area, my eyes land on the baby grand. I lower myself onto the bench and rest my hands on the ivories, taking in the opulence of the instrument. My fingers quickly find their home as I strike the keys to a familiar tune. I'm lost in the romantic melody of 'A Time for Us' when I hear a throat clear behind me. My fingers pause in place, before I begin again, not stopping until the last note dies out. I turn toward the woman behind me and we both smile. "That was the first song I learned."

She nodded. "I remember when you were first learning to play. I couldn't get you to do anything else. Your grades started slipping and the only thing that saved them was the threat that I'd sell the piano." She laughs. "Boy, that lit a fire under your feet. You made the honor roll every year after that." Nodding my head, another smile creeps over my face. Those were simpler times, when it had only been the two of us and that was all we needed to be happy.

Releasing a heavy sigh, I stand, and we make our way to the dining room where a gourmet feast is spread out on the antique pedestal table. Cook appears just as we sit, carrying a silver carafe and two porcelain cups on a glass tray.

"Thank you." My words carry an air of sincerity. I've never treated any staff member as a lesser individual. Humans are humans and we all need to feel appreciated from time to time.

After she pours our coffee and leaves the room, my eyes find my mother's. She quickly looks away and busies herself filling her plate with fruit, steadily avoiding my gaze. Finally, the silence gets the best of me. I grab her hand and give it a firm squeeze and her eyes swing back to mine.

"Mom, I didn't come here for the food." She's blinking at me like I've just insulted her.

"Then why did you come here, Julia?" Her words rush out with a force I'm not accustomed to from her. Swallowing the lump in my throat, I suddenly wish Ben was here with me.

"I need answers, Mom. Before you sling more bullshit about your parents, I want you to know I heard you talking to Marco last night."

Her face pales and her lips move, but no audible sound comes out. After a few minutes of silence, she replies. "Julia." That's it. That's all I get. I'm starting to get even more annoyed—if that's possible, when she continues. "You weren't supposed to know. It was the only way to keep you safe. How?" Shaking my head, I release her hand and see the anguish painted on her beautiful face.

"You must have accidentally dialed my number, and when I answered you couldn't hear me, but I heard you. What kind of documents were you talking about?" Her head hangs down like she's ashamed of what she's about to say. Shifting in her seat, the tears begin to form and she dabs at her eyes with a napkin.

"I don't know how to start." This time her tears are falling faster than she can blot them away and a faint groan escapes her lips as if she is in physical pain.

"God, Mom, is it that bad?" Now I'm terrified of what she's about to tell me. Do I really want to know what skeletons live in her closet? In our family's closet?

I move my chair so we sit side by side, and when she is able to pull her thoughts together, she replies. "Oh, Julia. I tried to make sure you never found out the truth about my family. I wanted to protect you at all costs."

I look at her and the color drains from my face. "What are you talking about, Mom? The time for keeping secrets is over. Just start from the beginning." As much as I need to know the truth, I'm realizing it could be much worse than any lie she's told.

Without speaking, she rises and I follow her into the den. She sits on the plush leather sofa while I claim the chair across from her. I hear a sharp intake of breath before her words pierce the air.

"When you were born, I gave you my mother's maiden name. At the time I'd already lost both parents and had little extended family." Determined to remain quiet now that she's talking, I nod my agreement instead of responding.

"You know my surname as Tolliver, but what you don't know is that the name is the anglicized version of Tagliaferro. Nikoli and Constance Tagliaferro were my parents. He was the head of the Italian mafia in New York at the time I was born.

I can't contain the gasp that spills from my mouth as she recounts her years under that roof. My anguished tears fall unashamedly when she tells me how her father pledged her to Carmine Baldoni when she was just sixteen years old. What started out as an arrangement ended up with them falling in love, although they never made it to the altar.

"It was a mess, really. Carmine was older than me by six years and for several years had a girlfriend his father did not like. To thwart that relationship, and at the same time forge an alliance with our family, Mr. Baldoni negotiated with my father and the result was an agreement that Carmine and I would marry."

"Did you meet Carmine before the agreement was made?"

"Don't be silly, Julia. You, of all people, know how these things work." My mother sighed and stroked the arm of the sofa a few times before continuing. "I met Carmine five months before the wedding and it surprised both of us how much we liked each other. He was very handsome, I was very naïve, and one thing led to another and I became pregnant. Then everything fell apart. Unbeknownst to my family and Mr. Baldoni, Carmine had fathered a son with his girlfriend—you know her as Maria." At my gasp, she answers my unspoken question, "Yes—the Maria who is now his wife."

My head spins as I struggle to put the pieces together. "Brando was the son?" My mother nods.

"Mr. Baldoni learned about Brando and broke the agreement with my father. When my father found out I was pregnant, he sent me away. He wanted a clean break with the Baldonis. When Carmine found out about my pregnancy, he tried to find me, but I was out of the country by then. He found us not long after you were born, but by that time it didn't matter because his father had forced Carmine to marry Maria."

My heart breaks for what she went through, although it isn't much different from my own experience. She spends the next hour recounting how her mother, when she found out what Nikoli had done, shot him in his sleep before turning the weapon on herself. Thankfully my mother had been sent away by then and didn't have to witness the violence.

After we've cried until there are no tears left, I pull away from our embrace and meet her eyes once again. "Mom, tell me about Marco. He's who I overheard you talking to last night. Is he connected to Michael?"

Her eyes suddenly light up like Christmas. "Oh my God, that's the most amazing part of all of this. Apparently your father had a second will buried in some bureaucratic bullshit. Marco always had a sweet spot where you and I were concerned, but no, he has nothing to do with Michael. I need you to trust me. Michael will never hurt you again. Marco called last week and told me about the will. Last night he urged me to tell you, but I was too afraid. Can you forgive me?"

"Oh Mom, of course I forgive you. But what's in the second will? How can we get our hands on it?"

"He's meeting with the executor, who has promised to help us by giving Marco access to the document."

I cut her off. "Do you trust Marco?"

"Explicitly. Marco is the one who convinced your father to leave us alone, on the condition that on your tenth birthday he'd have limited access to you. At the time I was in a lose/lose situation, and it was the best deal he would agree to." She sounds apologetic, the words ripped from her heart.

"So that's how I came to start visiting that house." I'm speaking to her but I'm staring out the window, focused on nothing.

"Oh, sweet girl, I had no idea how things would play out. I'll never forgive myself for not taking you and fleeing the country. But…"

She stops, and I finish her thought. "He'd find you. There was no place to hide, no escaping Carmine Baldoni. So, you did the only thing you could, you stayed." She nods silently and another tear slides down her cheek. I don't blame her, not really—she was just a scared young woman. And that's exactly how I escaped my marriage after I ultimately found the strength to leave. Although a lot of good that has done me given the recent developments.

I reach to wipe her tears when she pulls me into her embrace. When she releases me again, there's murder in her eyes.

"Julia, my love. Let's do it. Let's take down these motherfuckers once and for all."

I smiled. Who knew Katherine Tolliver was such a badass?

Chapter
TWENTY

Ben

It's just after three when Knight calls to tell me he's back in town. Tess has been managing the music store in his absence and he wants to check in to make sure his investment is still standing before he heads to the Lux to cover for me. I'm shaking my head. I don't understand their quirky relationship. I'm packed and ready to go before he arrives and shoot off a quick text.

> Me: Hey man, I'm going to head on out. Just call if you have an issue.

A response comes through immediately. It's just a middle finger emoji, which in King-speak is the equivalent of a thumbs up. Laughing to myself, I head out to the airport. Not wanting to wait for Courtland to send his plane back to Stone Creek to fetch me, I decided to fly coach for the first time in months.

As I suspected, my brother has a car waiting for me at JFK, even though I insisted it wasn't necessary. I slide into the back seat and the driver heads toward midtown. When we are a few blocks away, I pull out my phone to call Julia.

She picks up before the first full ring. She sounds excited. "Please tell me you're here." I chuckle because that's her signature greeting whenever I'm visiting the city.

"Nope, still in Stone Creek." I hear her deflated sigh, so I don't tease her for long.

"I'm kidding, Sunshine. I'm on my way to your place. Are you there?"

She huffs a groan. "Yes, I'm home. I just got back from seeing my mother. This conversation deserves a face-to-face. How close are you?"

"Here's an answer for you. You need to keep your blinds closed." She squeals, and the line goes dead. She's halfway down the sidewalk when I step out of the sedan and practically jumps into my arms.

We stand there, locked in a desperate embrace until a throat clears somewhere behind us. Turning, I see Courtland's driver with my bag in his hand. Letting go of Julia long enough to take the bag, we make our way to the door as the car pulls away.

As soon as we get inside, Julia pulls me to the sofa. "Don't move," she chirps. I watch as she goes to the bar and brings a bottle of Dom Perignon and two glasses to the table.

A coy smile touches the corner of my lips. "Sunshine, we've only been apart a few days. What are we celebrating?" She plops down beside me and tucks her legs underneath her as she waits for me to pour the bubbly. I hand her a glass and she smiles, her eyes twinkling with excitement.

"I have some killer news." I'm not sure if she is speaking literally or figuratively, although I'm hoping for the latter. It doesn't take long before I realize the figurative meaning of her words.

I listen as she reveals the things her mother admitted and my eyes widen when she explains how her father promised her to the Baldonis. But what I don't expect is the revelation about a second will. Hopefully, that will shed light on what steps we need to take to end this family's mob activities for good.

"So, when do we get to see this will?" My words ring doubtful even to myself, but we need to know the contents of the will in order to better fight Danny and his groupies.

"Marco is supposed to call Mom back with more information after he talks to the executor." She sounds optimistic. I just hope we get the information we need before it's too late. As if summoned by the mention of her name, Julia's phone rings. My eyes bounce from hers to her phone as she holds it up for me to see. It's Katherine.

She answers, her expression tense. I can't make out what's being said on the other end, but I'm watching Julia's expression change from pensive to elated in a matter of seconds. As she's listening to her mother, she grabs my phone, types out a message to me, and hands it back.

She talked to Marco. Wants to meet at The Brewery in an hour. We good to go?

I nod my head and call Courtland. After a few more exchanges, Julia ends the call just as Courtland picks up.

"Hey, Ben. You make it?"

"Yeah, a little while ago. Julia's mom has some interesting news. Can you meet us in an hour at The Brewery?"

"Sure thing. I'll send the car for you." Hanging up, I pull Julia into a hug, and toy with a strand of hair that has come loose from her ponytail. When I press her hand against my hard length, she giggles and shoves at my chest playfully.

"Ben, we don't have much time if we're going to be there in an hour. It's a twenty-minute drive through traffic." Groaning, I scrape my hand over my face.

"Sunshine, you're trying to kill me." Shaking my head, laughter still bubbles up.

"Trust me, big guy. No one has ever died from an unfulfilled erection."

"That you know of," I quip back.

After a ten minute back and forth that involves some heavy petting, we're on our way. Traffic is light tonight compared to other nights. I keep stealing glances at the gorgeous woman next to me when suddenly the vehicle begins to accelerate without warning.

My eyes snap up to Courtland's driver, who clearly appears tense, his eyes flicking between the road and the side mirror. "Is there a problem?" I'm immediately on high alert as he changes lanes and mutters a string of curses. "We're being followed."

Julia's head jerks up and I feel anxiety radiating off her in waves as we both turn to look behind us. The tinted glass provides just enough visibility for me to make out a black Escalade moving closer and gaining ground as we speed through the narrow streets. "Shit. Do you think Danny had someone watching my apartment?"

I'm cursing my decision to fly commercial when my gaze meets Julia's terrified expression. "Sunshine, I don't suppose you have your gun with you?" Grinning, she pulls the Glock from her purse and gives me a wink.

"You mean Ethel? I never leave home these days without her." As much as I want to give her shit for the ridiculous name, I'm grateful she's armed.

I take it from her hand and check the clip, then ask the driver, "Did you lose them?"

"Not sure, sir. I don't see them."

Before I can relax, thinking we've lost them, I see a dark vehicle approaching from the corner of my eye. *Shit.* Where did those fuckers come from?

As they pull alongside us, a hail of bullets erupts, hitting the side of the car and causing the driver to momentarily lose control before recovering. I manage to get off a few rounds, aiming for their tires. The Escalade begins to lose traction, and we pull away.

"Shit, man, that was crazy." Our driver's assessment echoes my thoughts. A few minutes later, we are sitting in front of the restaurant.

Luckily, we're only a few minutes late when we walk in to find Courtland, Molly, and Katherine sitting at a dimly lit table in the back. Three sets of eyes widen when they take in our appearance. Granted, our clothing is still pristine, but I'm sure our expressions tell a different story—which is evident when Courtland rises and meets us halfway.

"What happened?"

I can hear concern threaded in his voice. I have my arm wrapped around Julia and it tightens. "Let's sit first." Her steps are shaky as I lead her to the table, and we find our seats and order the strongest drink available. As soon as the waiter sets them in front of us, we look at each other, raise the glasses in a toast, and down them in their entirety.

Julia's mother is eyeing us with suspicion, but before she can ask what's going on, my brother's voice slices through the air.

"Ben, what the fuck happened?" He's clearly growing impatient with my stall tactics.

I'm still in a mild state of shock at the turn of events when I answer, "I'm not sure, but we're thankful for your driver. We were ambushed on the way over. The car took a hell of a beating before we were able to shake the assholes."

His blue eyes narrow and he cocks his head to the side. "Was it Baldoni?" What started out as concern has morphed into rage as he speaks.

"Probably. We didn't stick around to introduce ourselves, but given the current events, the chances of it being random are highly unlikely, yet not totally out of the question."

He nods his head in agreement. Then we all turn our attention to Katherine and Julia begins the questioning. "Mom, you said you had news from Marco. What did you find out?"

For the next hour we listen as Julia's mother explains the stipulations of the new will. It appears Carmine had this second one drawn up in case something like this played out and his idiot sons tried to pull this shit with Julia.

After we've finished eating and we are each nursing another sinfully hypnotic cocktail, Katherine drops the last truth bomb.

"The thing that makes this deal ironclad is the caveat." We all look at her, waiting to hear what this entails. She's looking at me as she speaks.

"You and Julia need to get married."

Chapter
TWENTY
ONE

Julia

"Beg pardon?" My eyes are saucers after my mother drops that bombshell. My mouth goes dry and I'm certain everyone can read my face. Married? I'm already married, though no one here except my mother knows that. I'm staring at her when I feel a firm hand on mine. When I look up, Ben has an odd expression on his face. Is that a smile playing over his mouth?

Shaking my head, I look at everyone at the table. All eyes are on me, and everyone else is smiling. "You're joking, right? Am I the only one here who thinks this idea is ludicrous? How is my getting married part of a deal to break free from the family for good?"

I make eye contact with my mother, and she nods her head, excitement lighting her eyes. Why does she not look horrified, knowing I can't possibly marry Ben?

"Yes, Julia. According to Carmine's second will, any instructions within it will supersede prior documents if you are married." Suddenly, a curtain of nausea rises in my throat and I struggle to keep it at bay.

"Have you seen this will? Can we trust it indeed exists?" I feel like I'm in some kind of alternate universe and my thoughts are reeling as I take in her words. I'm getting more anxious by the minute, and it doesn't ease even when Ben wraps his arm around my shoulder and pulls me in close. Molly and Courtland haven't said a word and that in itself has my nerves on edge. Curious to know what they're thinking, I direct my next question to Courtland.

"What are your thoughts? You've been awfully quiet." I should be addressing Ben, after all it's his future and life at stake as well, but I've always respected his brother's opinion. He clears his throat, and his eyes immediately dart to his twin.

"Look, if this will is authentic, then I think you should abide by it." I look at Ben, and relief appears to wash across his face. Of course, he wants his brother's input, but this is a decision that should be talked about and thought out.

Before I can respond, my mother interjects. "Julia, of course I viewed the document when I was at Marco's office this afternoon. It says that whatever was in his original will regarding retribution for past crimes is negated should you get married. As the head, the family can't touch you—and by extension, whomever you choose to marry, but this amendment has an expiration date."

I can't help my eye roll. "Of course, it does. What else is new?" I snort.

"If you and Ben are married within six months of learning of the new stipulation, you will both be untouchable."

Releasing a breath, I turn to Ben and give him a pleading look. As if reading my mind, he speaks. "Sunshine, I know you're worried, but this sounds like the best option. After we're married, we can be free of the rest of the Baldonis." If it were only that simple. How will a piece of paper protect us from the devil? If Danny, Joey, or Angie object to this second will, we're back to square one with no recourse. Not to mention, how are we going to skirt the issue of my current marriage? I release a heavy sigh as my eyes bounce around the table one more time. When my gaze meets my mother's, she gives me her signature head tilt, our secret communication that I need to trust her.

"Well, I guess we have a wedding to plan."

It's after ten when we arrive back at my apartment, and I can barely keep my eyes open as we make our way up the sidewalk. Handing Ben my keys, I watch as he unlocks the door and steps back for me to enter. I don't stop until I reach my bedroom, and pausing there only long enough to strip off my clothes. A smile curves my mouth as I sink into the softness of the plush mattress. Closing my eyes, I feel the bed dip as Ben joins me on the other side.

We haven't seen each other in days, and our quick interlude earlier was...incomplete, but I am beat, and he isn't making any moves to say otherwise. It's not long before I feel his arms wrap around me and I snuggle back against him. The last thing I remember before drifting off are soft hands threading through my hair and gentle kisses on the back of my neck.

"Please sit." Michael sweeps a large hand toward the spot next to him on the loveseat in the corner. My eyes drift to the floor and his shoes. Oh, God, they're big, too. Even though I'm not experienced sexually, I haven't been living in complete

darkness. I mean, I've heard the girls at school talk about male body parts, so everyone knows shoe size is directly linked to the size of his… Oh, God. If that's truly the case, then I'm royally fucked.

Like a fawn whose steps are tentative, I let shaky legs carry me across the room. I take a seat on the edge of the love seat, careful to keep a safe distance between us, but who am I kidding? There is no amount of distance that will maintain my safety. This man is dangerous. He may not look like it in his Armani tux and Italian leather shoes, but his charismatic smile hides the evil lurking just below the surface. Men like him, like my father, take what they want with or without permission. Although his demeanor is cool and detached, I know it's a matter of time before he pounces.

I'm trying to maintain my composure, but it's nearly impossible as my chest tightens, and my breathing becomes erratic. Just get it over with. Pressing my thighs together, I draw in a deep breath and meet his eyes again. They are dark, the striking blue from a few minutes ago has been replaced by two black pools. I can't look away as he takes my hand, tracing lines across my sweaty palm.

My cheeks flush and I look down, but he is quick to bring my focus back to his face. Holding my chin in place he levels me with those now-obsidian eyes and I'm suddenly relieved of all reason.

Time stands still. I'm pulled into a vacuum, isolated from everyone and everything. It doesn't register that he is moving me until the back of my knees hit the edge of the bed. I'm floating on a sensation of apprehension, but I'm also aware of rough hands on my shoulders turning me around until I'm facing the bed.

Cool fingers grasp the zipper of my dress, and I hear fabric parting until it pools on the floor around me. I'm standing in a white lace bra and panties. A low growl fills the air behind me, and I squeeze my eyes shut against the assault of hot breath on my ear.

"Beautiful." My arms hang limply as hands slowly move down my sides before stopping at my hips. He holds me in place and licks a trail from my ear to my shoulder, scorching my skin. An involuntary shudder rocks my body, and a gasp falls from my mouth.

I've never been touched like this before. It feels wrong. This is something to be shared between two people who care about each other. Not a lecherous old man looking to get off by ruining an untouched innocent. I blink back hot tears as I'm turned again and pushed down on the mattress, a hard body settling between my legs.

Somehow, during my mental fog, he had shed his trousers and boxers. He's wearing a white button down, the sleeves pushed to his elbows, and I glimpse his jacket casually thrown over the back of the loveseat. I'm still wearing the panties and bra, but I might as well be naked beneath him. When his hard length presses against my center and his hands cup my breasts, I want to disappear. The image of him hovering over my body is branded into my psyche and the smell of stale cigars and expensive bourbon makes my stomach lurch. I manage to hold back a gag as his tongue invades my mouth in a stolen kiss. His hands roam my most private parts, filling me with disgust as he plunders my body and takes what he wants with no regard for my wishes.

"Open your eyes, baby. I want to see them when I ruin you." His words are like poison darts aimed directly at my

heart, perfectly hitting their mark. He chuckles and I realize this is all a machination and I'm just a pawn in a bigger chess game.

"Let's get rid of the rest of these clothes, shall we?" Then I feel his hands, rough against the lace of my bra. A tug is all I feel at first, then with a rapid surge, he tears it down the middle—exposing me. My nipples immediately harden into stiff peaks from the breeze his movements create. Shame washes over me and I'm silently counting, trying to see how high I can get before this ends. His hands move from my breasts to my flat stomach, squeezing the tender flesh before traveling lower. Bracing himself on one arm, he grips the thin silk and I hear the unmistakable rip of fabric before another moan comes from his mouth, this one laced with what sounds like pain.

I really do try to obey him by keeping my eyes open, but on instinct they close. When I'm able to open them again, I concentrate on the ceiling and continue my count, although his weight on my chest keeps distracting me. I start to panic and focus on my breathing and give myself a mental pep talk.

Suddenly, his voice is a low rumble in my ear. "I'm going to take you, now. Try to relax, sweetheart," he growls in a rasping snarl. Tender words spoken with such contempt, it's like he's angry he has to do this. Squeezing my eyes tight as if to prevent this thing from happening, I hold my breath. My legs are pushed apart and something hot and hard breeches my entrance. It only goes in a little, but it feels like a serrated knife to my inner walls.

"Breathe, Julia." As if on command, the air is expelled from my lungs at the same time fire courses through my body. It feels like I'm being ripped in half. My body's reaction to this

foreign object is a silent scream to stop, but that's not what happens. I'm scrambling to get away, but the more I struggle, the deeper he seems to reach.

"I'm almost there. "Oh my God, almost there? How much more of him is there? Silent tears roll past my ears and fall onto the pillow. After a few agonizing moments, he stills. One arm clutches my hip while the other one keeps my shoulder pinned. "That's it. I'm in." That's it. Is it over? Relief courses through me, but it's short-lived when he speaks again.

"I'm going to start moving now. Remember to breathe." I open my eyes, and this time he's staring down at me, regret evident as his brow furrows. He pulls out, but it doesn't feel like all the way. There's still something embedded in my secret place. I press my lips into a tight line making sure I don't make a sound. I won't give him the satisfaction of knowing how this is affecting me. Before I can take a full breath, he plows back in. Without intending to, a yelp erupts from my mouth before I clamp it shut, clenching my teeth. He builds up a rhythm as powerful thrusts have my body inching upward on the mattress.

After several minutes that feel like a lifetime, his large body stills. Salty sweat drops slide down his forehead as his grunts and groans surround us. He holds me close to his body as he shudders his release. All I can do is take it. When he eventually pulls out and stands, his mouth forms a straight line.

"Fuck, I forgot a condom." I search his face, but all I find is a vicious smile—one that is hauntingly similar to the one I've grown accustomed to seeing on my father and brothers' faces. He lifts a shoulder and shrugs as if the possibility of him putting a baby inside his seventeen-year-old bride is just another business deal.

I'M SCREAMING FOR help when strong arms encircle me and pull me close. At first I fight back, until soft words tickle my ears. "Sunshine, shh it's okay. You had a nightmare." I'm gasping for air, thrashing about as he continues to whisper sweet nothings. I'm not deterred as I kick and claw my way to freedom. His hold on me tightens until finally I succumb to exhaustion and realize it's Ben that's comforting me and not a monster in my bed. Whimpers escape my mouth as he tucks me into his side and smooths my hair with soft hands. The tightness in my throat makes it difficult to speak.

He turns on the bedside lamp and I glimpse the crimson lines on his bicep. "Oh my God, Ben. I'm so sorry."

"Julia, don't apologize. I'm glad I was here for you." My accelerated heartbeat begins to slow and my breaths start to even out. I reach for his arm, but he pulls me in for a tight embrace. The darkness of the room is a perfect cloak to mask my face as I hide inside his arms. Tears track down my cheeks and I surrender to his touch. Rough fingers dance across my back until my eyelids flutter closed and sleep overtakes me again.

Chapter
TWENTY
TWO

Ben

Waking up next to the woman I love is always easy. Keeping my hands to myself is not so easy, but after the night we had, I want her to sleep in. So after quietly slipping out of the bedroom, I shuffle into the kitchen to start the coffee pot. Today is going to be an exhausting day of planning and strategizing.

I'm on the phone with my mom when I hear her enter the room. She leans in for a quick kiss then sits on the barstool next to me. My hand lands on her upper thigh. "I know, Mom. Things are really crazy right now, but my plan is to be back in Stone Creek by the weekend. Tell Dad I'll take care of it when I'm back or have Jack or Knight do it. He doesn't need to exert himself."

I listen as she relays his recent test results, which confirm the cancer is spreading. It isn't the news we were hoping for, but Robert King is a tough old bird. He won't stop until he has no other choice. I promise to check in later and end the call.

"How's your dad?" Julia asks, her voice a calming salve. I hadn't expected my mom's call this morning, so it took me by surprise. Standing up, I make my way over to the cupboard, grab two mugs and fill them with the steaming brew.

"His cancer is spreading. I don't know how much longer he'll be ambulatory and it's killing my mom, but she said this has been a good morning."

When I push a coffee mug in front of her, our eyes meet and tears gather in the corners of hers, making her brown eyes glow. Reaching up to wipe a stray tear from her cheek, she whispers. "Oh Ben. I'm so sorry," Those simple words could melt a frozen tundra. Quashing my own emotions, I walk back to my seat and pull her into my lap and try to change the subject. "That was some nightmare, huh?" She stiffens in my arms. When her troubled gaze meets mine, she simply nods and nuzzles my chest, and we remain locked in a silent embrace until a phone rings, hers this time. We'll revisit this conversation another time.

"Hello." She slides off my lap and her shoulders relax into easy conversation. She wipes her eyes and bites her lower lip. *I'd like to bite that lip.*

Relieved we aren't dealing with any drama this early, I decide to check in with Courtland. I'm leaning against the counter, coffee in one hand while I hear Julia recount the events from the night before. When Courtland doesn't answer my call, I decide to eavesdrop on Julia's conversation.

From what I gather, Molly has already phoned the girls and they've been making plans for an elaborate affair. Molly has appointed herself as our official wedding planner and Tess and Lucy are in charge of the food and photographer.

As happy as I am to be marrying Julia, the circumstances surrounding the ceremony have my senses heightened.

I continue listening as Julia's giggles saturate the room. Unfortunately for me, she places the call on speaker and that's my cue to leave. Before I can escape, Tess starts using the term she coined for us—Jul-Ben, which prompts a frown to form on Julia's face and her sunny expression turns serious. I don't catch Tess's words, but when Julia speaks there's concern in her voice. "What about Knight?" At the mention of my younger brother's name, my ears perk up. Julia gives her some type of encouraging acknowledgment before ending the call.

When she turns her attention to me, her face lights up with a smile that makes her eyes crinkle. I'm not sure what the last part of their conversation was about, but seeing her face takes away any anxiety I feel. "Sunshine, what's going on?"

A smirk touches the corner of her lips when she speaks. "Tess has a new boyfriend." Tess and my brother have a complicated relationship, and I knew it was just a matter of time before he lost his chance with her.

My brow arches as I read her mind. "Are you worried about my brother?" I can't blame her, I mean, all my brothers, including Knight, have fallen for Julia's friends.

"It's just… I always thought she and Knight were the perfect couple. And now…" She shrugs and I give her a lopsided grin. "We never know what the future holds for any of us."

Pulling her into a tight hug, my hands land on her backside and I give her cheeks a playful squeeze. When our eyes meet, desire is evident on her face, but she pulls back and shimmies out of my hold. "I'm hungry. What do you want for breakfast?"

"Oh, I have a few ideas." I hope my heated gaze conveys exactly what those ideas are, but if it does, she conveniently ignores it. I reach for her, but she darts away before I make contact.

Stalking toward her, I'm thinking about all the things I want to do to her gorgeous body, and when I finally grab her from behind and grind my erection against her tight ass, she squeals, and it sounds like an angel's song. "You asked what I wanted for breakfast. Let me show you." With that, I turn her around and lift her onto the granite countertop.

When I lift the oversize t-shirt she's wearing and push her legs apart, a growl emerges from my throat. "Fuck, Sunshine. No panties?" I'm humming my approval as I bend to meet her center. Using my hands I push her thighs further apart, I lower my head to her sweet pussy, taking a moment to inhale her unique scent. A subtle hint of jasmine hits my senses as my mouth finds her wet pussy, practically dripping with feminine juices; the flat of my tongue teases her most sensitive spot. Licking from back to front, I'm intoxicated by her sweet fragrance, and I never want to stop feasting on the sweetest pussy I've ever tasted.

I'm holding her still with both hands as I devour this decadent offering while she writhes and moans under the power of my mouth. When I sense she's on the edge, I slow my licks then lift my face to look at her, her juices most likely glistening on my chin, and I give a wicked chuckle.

"I swear to everything holy, Ben King, if you don't finish this, I'll never speak to you again." She's panting and her dark eyes are blazing with lust, making me grin like a crazy man. That's all the motivation I need to find her clit with my tongue and suck it into my mouth, letting my teeth gently graze the sensitive nub.

I increase the speed with which I feast and it only takes a minute before her legs are shaking and she tumbles over the edge into ecstasy, screaming my name.

By the time she recovers from her orgasmic haze, I have pushed my sweats down and am buried balls deep in heaven. She's clutching my shoulders when I pull out before thrusting back into her sweet heat, building up a rhythm that has me on the edge in minutes. After a few more deep thrusts, I'm spilling my seed into the woman who has my heart now and forever.

After a few breathless moments, we're both able to catch our breaths and when I pull away, she has a mischievous grin on her face. "What?" I can't help asking as a smile covers her beautiful face. I never want her to lose that smile. It's a smile that's reserved only for me, and I could be ready to fuck her again just from seeing it.

"King, did I ever tell you that you're a sex god?" I laugh quietly and meet her gaze. I set her to her feet and my fingers gently grip her chin and my other hand goes to her cheek. When I speak, there's a touch of humor in my words.

"Every damn day, Sunshine. Every damn day."

Chapter
TWENTY THREE

Julia

We fucked two more times before deciding to salvage what was left of this day. Not that a moment with Ben's huge cock buried inside me is ever a waste of time. Somehow, we managed to make it to the bedroom for the next round, and then into the shower—which obviously led to one more. Ben had taken me against the tiled wall and his brutal thrusts left me breathless and begging for more.

After we were clean and had come down from our post-sex high, Ben fed me pancakes. Yes, he actually forked each bite into my mouth as we sat side by side at the kitchen bar and he attended to my needs. Although I protested, he just laughed and assured me this is the way it is going to be. He said he won't have it any other way, so I'd better get used to the attention. But to me this goes beyond simple attention. Ben gives me what I didn't know I needed, but also what I'd never had before. When we are together, I feel cherished, like the most important woman in his world.

It's a crisp autumn day, so we dress quickly and set out to browse the familiar Fifth Avenue boutiques. October in Manhattan is a crapshoot. It is either hot or cold, and only rarely mild. Today proves to be that anomaly and we spend the afternoon riding bicycles in Central Park. It has been too long since we took time for ourselves, but when Ben suggested it earlier, I couldn't refuse.

We're midway through the park when my phone rings. We pull off the trail and find a soft patch of grass to sit on as I pluck my phone from my pocket. A smile forms on my face when I see the three boxes on the screen. Accepting them all at once, I'm looking at three very different scenes. Molly has her blonde hair in a messy bun, and she looks like she just rolled out of bed. Lucy's red locks are hanging in waves around her shoulders, and she looks freshly fucked. And of course Tess is Tess. Her blond hair is pulled back in a high ponytail and she looks like a girl who needs to be fucked. Obviously, my mind is still on sex and I laugh out loud. When they all look at me with puzzled expressions, I quickly compose myself and lie. "I'm sorry, Ben just said something funny."

Lucy is the first to speak. "So, Julia, what do you think about a double wedding?" My eyes brighten before my brows furrow into a deep frown. Hers and Jackson's wedding isn't for nine more months. We can't wait that long. In fact, even though the will said I had to get married within six months, we don't want to cut it too close, so we are thinking of four months from now. Maybe a Valentine's Day ceremony.

I'm not sure if Lucy or Tess know about the second will, and I decide on the spot to not say anything unless they mention it first. As far as I know, Molly is the only one who understands the situation and she won't say anything. I'm not trying to keep secrets from the two of them, but it's not something I enjoy talking about. I will let them know what's going on as soon as I'm ready, and until I'm ready, I don't want them asking too many questions.

I try to deflect the actual reason a double wedding won't work. "Oh, Lucy, you know you and Jack don't want to share the spotlight with us."

Her eyes narrow and realization dawns when she considers my words. "Oh my God, you're right. I never thought about it that way." She blinks back at me as her eyes dance with mirth.

Tess's bright eyes flutter with anticipation as she joins in the planning. "When did you say you'd be back in town? I'm watching the store for Knight for a few more days, but I don't have anything after next Sunday." I glimpse Lucy roll her eyes at our friend.

"Okay, Lucy, spill it. What's going on with the eye roll?" Her response is another eye roll before she launches into her explanation. "Tess is in love." Lucy can't help herself and Molly's laugh is infectious.

"Oh my God, Lucy, I'm not in love. Dillon and I are taking it slow. We've both come out of relationships and we're just finding our way."

"Dillon, huh? Nice name." I smirk, shaking my head as I turn my attention back to Tess's question. "We have some things to wrap up in the city, but I'm hoping to be back in Stone Creek by Friday." That's the tentative plan, anyway.

"So, if you and Ben are tying the knot, it must mean whatever shit you have going on with your brother is handled, correct?" Tess has a look of concern etched on her face.

"Something like that." I give a weak smile and after promising to keep them in the loop, the call ends. When I look over at Ben, he grins and those dimples—my God, the man is magical. "Is something funny, Sir?"

His nostrils flare and his eyes radiate heat. "I love it when you call me sir."

Now it's my turn to roll my eyes. "Down boy." When I laugh, he cocks his head and pulls me into an embrace, completely unconcerned by the crowd that has formed around us. After a few sated moments, I pull away and stab at my phone.

"Before we get on with our ride, I need to check in with my mother." Typing out a text, I hit send and wait for her response.

> Me: Hey, Mom. Just checking in. Ben and I are out and about. I'll call you later.

Almost immediately, the word bubble appears on the screen and her message comes through.

> Mom: Julia, darling, enjoy your day with Ben. I look forward to your call later. xoxo

Smiling, I tuck the phone back in my pocket, and we finish our ride. By the time we arrive back at my apartment, the late afternoon sun has started painting shadows on the buildings. We're laughing and talking when we reach the front step. A cold chill sweeps over me when I see the front door slightly ajar. I can't get words past my tight throat, so I turn and point.

Ben extends his arm and ushers me to move behind him. I'm clutching his shoulders as he leads the way inside. As soon as we cross the threshold, I'm stopped in my tracks. My apartment is in shambles, not one piece of furniture remains untouched, my paintings are slashed, and glassware has been shattered.

"Don't touch anything." Ben whispers as he takes his phone from his pocket and dials 911. I'm moving in a fog, tiptoeing through piles of debris. I carefully make my way toward the bedroom, and when I open the door, a scream escapes my mouth. My mattress has been ripped at the seams and my pillows slashed—the room is littered with feathers. All my clothing is stripped from the bureau drawers and scattered across the room, and a deep heaviness settles in my chest. As devastating as this is, what I see next is what pushes me over the edge and a gasp is pulled from my lips.

On the mirror above my dresser is a photo of Ben. My fingers hover over the image, but I'm careful not to touch it. This was taken today. He's wearing the same fucking clothes he has on now. What fills my veins with ice are the images of his eyes scratched out and something red smeared across his body. Below the picture, written on the mirror in red lipstick, are words that destroy my heart.

Don't fight the family. You'll never win.

Chapter
TWENTY
FOUR

Julia

After the police arrive and collect the evidence, Ben books a suite at the Plaza for the night. I can't return to the apartment until the authorities determine if they need anything else to further the investigation. My mind is racing, and my nerves are shot. We need to expedite this amendment to my father's will and this wedding needs to take place as soon as possible.

Apparently Danny wasn't bluffing, and my heart is in pieces as I think about Ben and what my brother will do if we don't stop him. Although the police who came to my apartment seemed competent, I know that ultimately they will be of little use as the family has had key players in each department in their pockets for years. We'll have to beat Danny at his own game. The line has been drawn in the sand and whoever crosses it first, wins.

I'm watching Ben as he stands looking out the hotel windows, one fist clenched and the other clutching a whiskey glass. Suddenly the glass makes contact with the wall and a shout bursts from his mouth.

"Motherfucker." I yelp at the unexpected sound. He jerks his head toward me, his face a mask of defeat.

"I'm sorry, Sunshine, I didn't know you were in here." Grabbing a towel from the bathroom, I wipe up the amber liquid and inspect his hand for potential cuts. When I find none, I wrap my arms around his neck; his hands move to my hips and he gives them a possessive squeeze.

Taking his hands in mine, I pull us to the bed and crawl onto the plush down comforter, taking him with me. We're sitting opposite one another, but still close enough for me to take his face in my hands, his stubble rough to the touch.

Looking into his dark eyes, I'm searching for something to say that will make all the bad disappear, but I can't find the words. Thankfully, he saves me by saying what I can't articulate. "Sunshine, I promise it's going to be okay. Danny won't touch us." I look at him, my face wet with tears. How can he be so certain things will work out when the threats are getting closer?

I move off the bed, suddenly needing to put distance between us. "Ben, don't make promises you can't keep."

I'm silently pleading with him to open his eyes and realize the magnitude of what we're dealing with. I turn to look outside, and I feel his warm breath on my neck. "Look at me, Julia."

It's almost a whisper and my head snaps up at his use of my given name. I move closer as he tucks a strand of hair behind my ear and presses his lips to mine. When he pulls back and looks into my eyes, I'm a sex-crazed mess and I need to clutch his shoulders to remain upright.

He senses my body's reaction and laughs. "Sweetheart, trust me. We will take down the Baldonis with or without the marriage amendment." His words make me think things I have no business thinking. They make me hope when I have no hope left. I have to end this with my family once and for all. These blatant threats are hitting closer each time, their violence escalating. It won't be long before hell will be at our doorstep. There's no escaping it. I'm the only one who can stop it.

It's after ten, but Ben has arranged to meet Courtland. As soon as he leaves, I grab my phone and press the button, connecting me to the devil himself. When I hear his voice, my stomach rolls and I'm hit with a sudden wave of nausea. Lifting my head, I find my courage and speak.

"Clear your schedule. I'm on my way over to offer you a deal." I quickly end the call. I don't give him a chance to make excuses. I don't have time for his shit, not now.

I feel cold sweat forming on my neck, and I rush to the bathroom and fall to my knees in front of the toilet. I'm not sure how long I kneel on the floor before the dry heaves finally stop. Reaching for the counter, I pull myself up and gasp when I take in my reflection. My skin is pale, and dark circles hang under my eyes. I wash my face before applying make-up and pull my hair into a small chignon.

I order a car and then slip on my red linen dress and black pumps, thankful that the officers let me take them, because the outfit screams power. If Danny so desperately wants me to lead the family, that's what I'll fucking do, but he'll soon find out my loyalty comes with a steep price.

The car is waiting when I step out of the hotel lobby. Giving the driver the address, I settle back in the seat and watch as the city passes by. We drive down the streets of Manhattan for twenty minutes before we pull up to the gated entrance of the opulent Baldoni family mansion. I haven't been back here willingly since the night I was married. Even when my father died, I didn't return. Only one thing has the power to get me here voluntarily—fear for the man I love.

That's the only reason I have made this decision—I just pray Danny accepts it without a fight. There's a good chance he'll laugh in my face at what I'm proposing, but I'll never know if I don't try.

When the car stops, I remain in the seat. Suddenly the courage I had summoned when I made that call to Danny wanes and fear meets me like a slap to the face. After a couple of minutes, the driver appears, opening the back door to usher me out. His movement shocks me back to reality and I find myself at the threshold of the Baldoni Compound.

My hand is poised to knock when the door opens and my brother is standing there, except it isn't Danny. Joey shifts nervously on his feet as he takes in my appearance before stepping aside and allowing me to enter. "Joey."

He nods his head in greeting, and I step past him before turning to meet his gaze. "Where is he?" He knows who I'm talking about. I'm here to make a deal with the devil and the only currency that will be accepted is my soul. I walk through the open foyer, each step weighing like a millstone, until I stop in front of the stone fireplace and focus on the picture that hangs above the mantle.

A portrait of my father graces the stone. He is younger, possibly thirty at the time. Searching his face for some resemblance, I see my three brothers reflected in his eyes, but Angie and I take solely after our mothers. Only DNA binds us together.

Turning slightly, Joey is standing by my side. He offers me a drink, which I decline. This isn't a social call, I'm here for business.

"There you are." I know his voice before I see his face. Joey turns to leave, but I place a hand on his shoulder indicating he should stay. Better to have a reliable witness in the room than to count on Danny's stellar integrity. I can just see him agreeing to my demands now, only to blindside me later.

When I glance at Joey, he looks agitated. Whatever is going on between the two of them, I don't want to get in the middle. "Hello, Daniel." Keeping my words clipped, I move to face both brothers. Danny smirks and moves closer to me before responding. "So Julia Bear, let's talk about this deal you're offering me." His voice sounds cold and detached as he crowds me. I know his intimidation tactics well. If he thinks I'll shrink back in fear, he has another thing coming.

Resisting the urge to step back, I cross my arms over my chest and meet his gaze. I can give as good as he can.

After he realizes I'm not backing down, Danny finally steps back and sits on the sofa. He sweeps his arm out in a grand gesture for me to join him. I roll my eyes and shake my head.

"Thank you, but I'd rather stand." Wandering to the window, I look out over the grounds. Although it's dark this late at night, I remember the splendor of the lush rolling hills in the distance. New lights, probably solar, illuminate the old koi pond just beyond the courtyard, and a memory surfaces of sitting at its edge, reading. To an outsider, this looks like a happy, thriving home where a family loves and protects one another. But I know the ugly secrets buried within these walls. Only my love for Ben will keep me here. If sacrificing myself will spare his life, I'll do it a million times over. I'm at the water's edge. It's time to sink or swim.

I force the words past my lips before I change my mind. "I'll do it. I'll take my place in the family on one condition."

Before I can finish, Danny cuts me off. "I'd no doubt there would be a condition. Let me guess, you'll lead the family in exchange for Loverboy's life." At this moment I've never hated anyone more in my life. His evil grin makes my skin crawl and once again I think I'm going to be sick, but I swallow the bile rising in my throat and raise my chin in utter defiance.

What could I say? He knew what my condition would be. He knew the only way I'd agree was if Ben's life was spared. "That's exactly what I want." I spit out angrily as I watch his demeanor change from cocky to dangerous in a split second.

"Do you really believe Ben King will be safe if you're the boss? Sometimes the family's employees have issues falling under certain controls. Loyalty only goes so far." My hold on my anger is slipping at his arrogant question.

"What the fuck does that mean, Danny?" I swear if I'd brought my gun, this fucker would be dead right now. He is testing me, and I'm about to go nuclear on his ass.

He holds my gaze for a moment before holding up his hands in defense. "Relax, little girl. If King means enough to you to give up your freedom, then we have a deal." He has the audacity to hold out his hand as if I'd touch his smarmy skin.

I snort out a response, my words lethal. "If he so much as gets a hangnail, I'll put a bullet between your eyes."

Yeah, motherfucker, and I have a witness to attest to it. Danny flinches, as if I'd struck him, then laughs. "Such violence." His mocking tone has my body tensing as I try to rein in my emotions.

I'm already on edge and the more he baits me, the closer I am to losing this battle, not to mention the war. I'm determined to keep Ben safe, so I pull out the envelope I had delivered to me before I left the hotel. Shoving it in his face, he looks up at me before reaching for it. "What's this?" He sounds nervous, unlike the calculating bastard I've always known.

I can't help the smirk that touches my mouth. "Just an insurance policy, little brother. You didn't think I'd simply take your word for anything, did you?"

He stares at the envelope longer than expected and when his eyes meet mine again, his face displays exactly what I wanted. Pure hatred radiates from his body as he tears it open and extracts the contents. He scans the document before jumping to his feet and uttering a string of curses.

The grin that overtakes my lips seems to touch my entire face. *Checkmate, Danny.* Apparently, the contract I had drawn up wasn't part of his insidious plan, but I had finally beat him at his own game even if it cost me the man I love.

Reaching across the mahogany desk, I pluck a pen from its holder and hold it out to him. "Sign it, brother, and you can claim victory." I stand, holding the pen while simultaneously holding my breath. When his fingers close around the cool metal, I quietly release the breath I've been holding and step back. My mind is a whirlwind of thoughts as I hear the pen scrape across the paper before he throws both the pen and the paper to the floor and stalks out of the room, slamming the door behind him.

Now that it's done, and Ben's life is secure, I'm faced with the unthinkable task of delivering the devastating blow.

As I am about to leave, my phone beeps with a voice message. Funny, I never heard it ring. Putting the phone to my ear, I listen as the officer in charge of investigating the break-in informs me I can return to my apartment whenever I am ready because they have what they need as evidence. An act which was pointless, considering we know who was responsible, but I just breathe a sigh of relief, offer a quick goodbye to Joey, and leave to sort through the chaos that is my life.

I don't even remember the ride back into town, and it's only when the car pulls to a stop that I realize I'm home. Well, at least until I move into the mansion, after I seal this deal and once again become a puppet on a string. Although I'm supposed to be the one calling the shots, I'm essentially a mouthpiece doing Danny's bidding and I have no one to blame but myself.

I stand for a long time before opening the door and shuffling inside. The room looks like a demolition site. I slowly make my way into the kitchen to grab a trash bag. The hope that someone would take responsibility for cleaning this mess is futile, but what I wouldn't give for a fairy godmother appearing and plucking me up to drop me in an alternate universe. A universe where the Baldonis don't exist and Ben and I can live out our days in uninterrupted carnal bliss. Alas, there is no fairy godmother to change my reality.

Pulling on a pair of kitchen gloves, I take the bag and set about clearing debris from the floor. A pang of sadness hits me like a sledgehammer as I gather the fragments of my most treasured art—irreplaceable canvases that held pieces of my heart. When I move to the bedroom, I'm thankful that the defaced picture of Ben is nowhere to be seen. Assuming it was part of the evidence collection, I continue sorting through anything salvageable before tossing the rest.

When I finally tie the last bag three hours later, the apartment looks somewhat normal and there are six trash bags filled with my worldly possessions.

Of all my belongings, I will most miss my childhood mattress. My mother had it specially made for me when I turned thirteen and I have moved it with me multiple times, including to Juilliard while I was studying there. Silent tears slip down my face for what I've lost—the tangible items and my future. That last one is bone crushing.

After dragging the bags to the curb to be picked up, I jump in the shower hoping to wash away the sadness along with the grit and grime. Reaching for the body wash, I choose the subtle scent of teakwood and spice that Ben keeps on "his" shelf in the shower. As I smooth the creamy gel over my heated skin, I allow the tears to fall again, but this time they are anything but silent.

"Fuck, fuck, fuck." I'm wailing and every inch of my body aches. Even my eyeballs burn as if they've been stabbed with scorching skewers. My body is wrecked and I know I can't fight any longer. Yes, my mother convinced me and Ben that marriage would save us, but after the last stunt Danny pulled, I can't gamble with Ben's life that way. He will most likely hate me after everything is said and done, but at least he'll be alive to do it.

When the water finally turns cold, I step out of the shower and wrap an oversized towel around my body. Padding back into my bedroom in search of something to wear, I choose a pair of distressed jeans, an off the shoulder argyle sweater and a pair of red Chuck Taylors. I look at my phone and see two missed calls from Ben's number.

I know if I hear his voice, I'll be powerless to do what has to be done, so instead of calling him, I send a quick text telling him that I've returned to the apartment and that I'd like to meet up with him later.

My heart is in my hands and I can barely catch my breath when I hit send. A message appears almost immediately.

> Ben: Still meeting with Courtland's team. Almost done. I'll call you then.

I simply send a thumbs up before dropping my phone on the bar. My heart is breaking as I sit with my head in my hands and think about what's to come.

Knowing I'm about to shatter both our worlds, I slide off the barstool and wander to the counter, opening the top drawer and grabbing stationary and a pen. This simple paper and pen feel like a betrayal of epic proportions, but I can't stop myself once the words begin to flow.

After an hour and several balled up pieces of paper tossed to the floor, I've crafted the perfect break-up letter. Yes, Ben King deserves more than my broken words as I try to soften the blow, but in my heart nothing can ease the pain my words will cause. I need to make him hate me.

My head is aching from the ugly tears I've cried through this process and I feel as though I'm going to be sick. I slide the letter into a scented envelope and place it on the table where he is sure to see it, next to the legal folder that will solidify his hatred.

I'm just about to walk out the door when my phone rings. Seeing his name flash across the screen sends another pang of guilt through my body. I silence my phone, tuck it in my purse, and walk out the door.

He will be here soon. He'll see the letter and hopefully I'll have hit my mark. He needs to hate me in order to stay safe. Nothing else in the world matters. I have sacrificed myself for the man I love and I refuse to regret it.

Chapter
TWENTY FIVE

Ben

The ring burns a hole in my jacket pocket. I saw it in a jewelry store window while we were in New York last week. The way the light bounced off the emerald cut diamond made it impossible to resist. Pulling the velvet box from my pocket, I take the ring in my fingers, imagining how it will look on her hand. Tonight will be the perfect time to pop the question. With everything going on in our lives, we need something beautiful to look forward to. Picking up my phone, I call her number to let her know I'm almost there.

I'm beginning to worry, because she hasn't picked up any of my calls. It's midafternoon when the driver turns onto her street, and I practically jump out of the moving vehicle, desperate to find her.

Taking the steps two at a time, I'm clutching the key she gave me months ago like it's a lifeline while a myriad of scenarios run through my head. Thoughts of her possibly being hurt or… I won't go there. There has to be a logical explanation for her being off the grid, but nothing rational comes to mind. The idea of anyone hurting her has my heart racing and my blood boiling.

Opening the door with more force than necessary, I'm met with silence. It's quiet, too quiet. Her presence invades any space she occupies and right now my senses tell me she's gone.

I look around and see that she has cleaned most of the mess up. My eyes land on the table—and an envelope. Making my way toward it, I see that the envelope is addressed to me. There's a folder beside it. My heartbeat accelerates and a sick feeling washes over me as I pick up the envelope with shaky fingers and sink into the closest chair. Swallowing the lump in my throat, I slide the paper out and blow out a long exhale.

My fingers tighten around the edges as the words appear in front of me.

> My Dearest Ben,
>
> This is by far the hardest thing I've ever had to do. But I know I'm doing the right thing, and I hope one day you'll understand.

My hands are shaking, making it difficult to read her words or maybe it's the moisture pooling in my eyes. I close my eyes, and tears leak down my cheeks. I feel like I'm being ripped in two. After a moment, I open my eyes. The words are swimming on the page until I blot my eyes with my hands.

> My place is with the family. I've fought too long against the inevitable and I can no longer fight it. I will be moving to the mansion soon. Please don't follow me, it will only make it harder for both of us. The evidence in the folder will tell the rest of my story. I'm too much of a coward to face you, so please respect my decision. I'll never forget you and I'll love you forever.
>
> Your Sunshine

My vision clouds and there's a roar in my ears as my fingers coast across the smooth page. I'm paralyzed as I read the words again. This can't be real. This isn't Julia. She's tough as nails, but she wouldn't be callous enough to write me a Dear John letter. Not after everything we've been through. By the time I've read the letter for the third time, I'm convinced Danny is behind it. That's the only sane explanation, as if anything about this situation could be considered sane. I grab the folder from the table, and in my haste the contents fall out. My eyes land on the title page as I sink to the floor. It's a marriage certificate.

Julia Elizabeth Bernard Baldoni and Michael Lorenzo Singara
were married on December eighth in the year of our Lord…

Letting the paper fall from my hands, I manage to pull myself up and rush to the bathroom in time to collapse in front of the toilet, expelling the contents of my demolished world. When the curtain of nausea finally subsides, I stagger back to the dining room. With shaky fingers, I pick up the document and sink back onto the chair.

I need answers. I need to hear this from her mouth before I believe it's real. Pushing down my throbbing headache, I grab my phone and stab her number. It immediately goes to voicemail. My first instinct is to hang up. After her sunny greeting, I manage a sharp intake of air and speak, the words rushing from my mouth, like if I don't say them quickly, they will disappear.

"Sunshine, call me, please. We need to talk about this. There's always another way."

After I cut the call, my eyes linger on the papers in front of me. There has to be an explanation. Married? How can she be married? *We* were going to be married. This is not the end. I will die before I let her give up on us.

I'm losing my mind by the time I decide to call Molly. She picks up almost immediately.

"Hey, Molly, have you heard from Julia today? I'm a little worried she hasn't returned any of my calls." I conveniently leave out the heart shattering letter she left.

The line is quiet for a beat before she answers. "No, I'm sorry Ben. I haven't talked to her since yesterday. Do you think something happened with her brother?" There's an edge of concern in her voice. I don't want to jump to any unnecessary conclusions, so I downplay my next words.

"I'm sure she's just shopping or something and forgot her phone, but if you hear from her, would you let her know to call me?"

"Sure thing, Ben." As soon as the call ends, I punch in Courtland's number. After two rings his cool voice comes through the phone.

"I thought you'd be balls deep in wedding planning this afternoon."

His offhand comment hits me the wrong way and I react. "I don't have time to dick around, Courtland."

"What's going on?" His demeanor turns serious, and he knows I'm not fooling around.

"Julia's missing." There's a bite to my words.

"Missing? What do you mean?"

I huff in response, annoyed by his ridiculous questions. "What do you think it means? She's missing, as if she walked off the face of the earth." Maybe I'm being overly dramatic, but with everything going on with that fucked up family of hers, nothing would surprise me.

Taking a few deep breaths, I'm suddenly hit with a wave of guilt. My brother isn't the enemy. The only villain in this scenario is Danny Baldoni and anyone stupid enough to have a death wish.

When I speak again, my words aren't quite as sharp. "I'm sorry, man. It's just I can't get in touch with her, and she left a letter in her apartment."

I can feel his frustration building. "A letter? What kind of letter?"

I actually laugh at the question because it's ridiculous to think she really wants this. Tamping that emotion down, I try to keep my words even. "She says she's taking over the family. That it's her place in life and for me not to follow her."

"What about the wedding? What changed her mind?" The suspicion in his words tells me we were on the same page.

"Fuck if I know, but…" I break off when I hear some type of commotion in the background. He must be at his office.

"Oh fuck. This is bad."

"What?" I bite out, annoyed with my brother's theatrics.

"Um, brother. Turn on Channel 3 news. You have to see this." Keeping him on the phone, I move to the TV, grab the remote and when the screen appears, my heart practically stops. There, in front of my eyes is the woman I love, flanked by her two brothers. Her sister stands to the left of Joey. There's a man who I recognize as Liam Black, Carmine's personal bodyguard standing next to Angie.

"Shit." I'm immovable, incapable of further speech. Courtland's voice slices through the air.

"Ben, are you there?" It takes a minute to find my voice, but when I do, I can only manage a whisper.

"Yeah, I'm here." Neither of us speaks again as we take in the scene before us. All four Baldoni siblings stand together—Julia is behind a podium, speaking into a microphone. I'm mesmerized as she talks, taking in every nuance, every movement, looking for any crack in her carefully constructed facade. Her dark coffee eyes appear vacant and her robotic voice drones on as if her entire speech is scripted. I'm not even sure I'm breathing, as I'm captivated by her words. She's dressed as a power player in a dark gray pencil skirt with matching blazer.

It's hard to keep up with her words when I'm grappling with the images playing out on the screen. It seems I catch every other word. Family, importance, loyalty, power, determination.

Finally, I give up completely when the camera zooms in for a closeup. Her face is stoic, but her eyes tell a different story. What may not be noticeable to others is a glaring beacon to me. A lone tear sits on the edge of one eye until her slender finger reaches up to wipe it away.

My words are trapped in my throat, so I'm thankful when my brother breaks the silence. "Jesus fucking Christ. Do you believe that shit?" I feel as if all the blood has drained from my body as I clear my throat and attempt to answer.

"I really don't know what to believe anymore, but until just now I would have bet everything I owned and more that Danny was the source of this travesty. But now I'm just not sure, brother."

After I hang up, I try Julia's cell again. After three rings the call connects and I'm waiting to hear her soft voice, but that's not what greets me on the other end. "King." I'd know that sickening voice anywhere and I won't give him the time of day.

"Where's Julia? I need to talk to her." I try to keep the desperation out of my voice as I speak.

"Benjamin, Benjamin, Benjamin. Didn't Julia make herself clear in her love note, oh wait, it was a break-up letter. Or did her marriage certificate seal the deal?" He chuckles and I want to reach through the phone and rip his fucking tongue out. He doesn't deserve to speak her name.

"Just put her on the phone. I only need a minute." There is no way he can miss my ire—I'm sure it's coming through loud and clear.

"No can do, King. You see, Ms. Baldoni is in a meeting and cannot be disturbed. But, if you'd like to leave a number, I can tell her you called. I'm sure she'll get to your call eventually." I am getting nowhere with this smug son of a bitch, so I stab the end button. For extra emphasis, I slam my phone against the wall, the force shattering the screen on impact.

"Motherfucker!" My hands are tied if I can't talk to her. I have to find out why this is happening. The second will is supposed to be ironclad and includes the marriage amendment that is supposed to be our trump card.

So many questions are spinning in my head. Is she being coerced into this arrangement? Is the pull to lead the family so strong that it was worth ending our relationship? How could she be married without me having a clue? These are questions I need answers to, and she is the only one I trust to provide them. Getting access to her will be tricky and after Danny intercepted my call, I'm certain he'll be even more determined to keep her hidden away.

As if this shit show isn't enough to bring me to my knees, I have to face the fact that I am needed back in Stone Creek. I can't rely on my brothers' generosity much longer when it comes to managing the Lux—they both have their own businesses and responsibilities to handle. And then there's the issue of our dad's health.

I decide to stay in Manhattan until tomorrow afternoon. If I haven't made contact with Julia by then, I will have no other choice but to go home, at least for a few days.

I'm sitting on the front porch of her apartment long after the sun has set, picturing shadows of pink and purple painting the night sky. That's the way the sunset looks in Stone Creek. Here in the city?

You're lucky if you glimpse a dozen stars as streetlights and city lights block out Mother Nature's offerings.

My eyes are fixed on her door, but it remains closed and dark, the only light coming from the lone sconce by the sidewalk. It's after midnight when I decide she's not coming back, at least not tonight, so I make my way back to the hotel.

I strip off my clothes and fall into bed, mentally exhausted from the events of the day. After tossing and turning for a while, I finally sink into a fitful sleep, only to wake up three hours later. Swinging my legs off the bed, I traipse to the bathroom for a shower. The clock says five o'clock, too early to call anyone except Courtland, but I doubt he has any relevant news this early in the morning.

After my shower, I dress in loose gray joggers and a worn black t-shirt. I'm headed to the lobby to get coffee and something to eat when my phone rings. I grab it on the first ring.

"Talk to me, Courtland." I'm anxious to hear what his contacts found out last night.

"Hey man. I just got off the phone with my head of security. They were able to get a bug planted inside the Baldoni mansion without incident."

"Thank fuck. So, what now?" My chest tightens just hearing that name. If I could go back in time, before any of this shit happened, I would have never let Jackson agree to this blackmail. When Brando and Danny had started spouting their big dick energy, I'd have found a way to end all the fuckers. But the old Ben was weak. He hadn't yet experienced the love of a good woman.

That gentle Ben exists no more. In his place is a Brutal Prince. My brothers always called me Prince because I was the firstborn, the King's son. Courtland followed two minutes later. The nickname stuck with me for years, but died away when we became adults. Now it might be time to resurrect it.

I listen as my brother relays how his security team set up surveillance not far from the mansion. I'm looking around nervously, making sure there aren't any eyes or ears close by.

"Are you sure it's secure? What are the chances they were detected?"

"Relax, I know you're worked up and for a good reason, but trust me, they're the best."

"You don't understand; there's more. It appears Julia got married when she was seventeen." I hear the sharp intake of breath. "Yeah, it was a shock to me, too. She left the documents along with the letter. There's got to be more to it."

After a few more assurances, we end the call. Pulling up our thread, I fire off a text. If she answers, she answers. I've got nothing to lose at this point.

> Me: Hey, Sunshine. I need to see you. Can we meet somewhere private?

I'm still in the lobby, on my third cup of coffee, when my phone pings and I almost spill the whole damn cup trying to get to my phone. My heart leaps when I see her name on the screen, but it's immediately destroyed when I read her message.

> Julia: Hello, Ben. I don't think that would be a very wise idea. It's time to say goodbye.

I stare at my phone like the words will magically change until the waitress brings my food. I look at the plate of gourmet pastries, bacon, sausage, and eggs and my vision blurs, while my insides feel like they're being twisted into a pretzel.

I take a few calming breaths and manage to eat a small pastry and a few bites of egg before dragging myself back to the room. Courtland told me it would be too risky for me to be seen close to the surveillance van, but I could set up in his office where we'd be able to connect with the team.

I change quickly and step outside as the Uber I ordered comes to a stop. I spend the car ride staring at my phone, willing Julia to call, to tell me this is all a cosmic joke, but by the time we pull up to King Enterprises, there's been no call, no text. Tucking the phone in my jacket pocket, I emerge from the car and make my way inside, mustering a smile for the receptionist, and make my way to the bank of elevators.

It's only ten in the morning, but when I walk through the beveled glass doors, Courtland is sitting behind his desk with a cut glass decanter and two glasses in front of him. He nods toward the chair that faces his desk, and I take a seat as he places ice in the glasses then pours what I know to be an expensive Scotch into both glasses before sliding one my direction.

My brother is larger than life and at this moment he is my lifeline. He has the type of pull I'll never acquire in the business world. The kind that can take down a family as powerful as the Baldonis.

We don't speak at first. I just savor the amber liquid and the comfortable burn that coats my throat and clears my mind—and give thanks that I managed to eat a little breakfast.

After we've finished our drinks, he pours us each another and begins pressing buttons on his computer. The connection appears grainy then a male voice can be heard across the line. I hold my breath before Courtland smirks.

"They can't hear us. You don't have to be quiet." His words hold promise. He wants me to be free to express how I feel at this turn of events. I'm leaning forward so as to not miss a word when Danny drops the first truth bomb.

"Yeah, she thinks she sacrificed herself to save that piece of shit King, but she has no idea, does she?"

There's silence. He must be on a call, and I can't hear the other person. Who is he speaking to? I'm not sure we'll get enough from a one-sided conversation and tension wracks my body.

I look at Courtland and he shrugs. "From here we'll only be able to hear whoever is in the mansion." He must see the immediate defeat on my face because he continues. "But the van will be picking up both sides." A wave of relief washes over me as I turn my attention back to what Danny's talking about.

"Trust me, I've got it all worked out. I've requisitioned the money. She won't see it coming. Yeah that little bitch thinks the family lawyer is on her side." He laughs and I wince. I'd like to get my hands around his neck. White hot rage has my blood boiling.

"Tomorrow night. It's handled." Then the line goes dead as Courtland picks up his phone and presses a button.

"Yeah, Boss." The voice sounds muffled like it's coming from far away.

"Did you get everything?" His voice is cold, detached. This is pre-Molly Courtland, and he is as ruthless as ever. There's a long pause on the other end before another voice comes on the line, this one clearer.

"Uh, hello, Sir. From what we heard, it was another man he was talking to. Liam Black, Sir."

Liam? What the hell? He was Carmine Baldoni's most respected bodyguard, loyal to a fault.

I refrain from blowing my top, not wanting to miss anything that's being said. "I see. How soon can you get the transcripts here?" He sounds irritated as he speaks.

"I can have Stan drive them over in about an hour. Do you want to maintain surveillance throughout today?"

"That's what I'm paying you for." His temper is beginning to make an appearance, and I am right there with him.

"Right. Okay, Sir. We'll keep you posted." With that, the call ends. I'm blinking at my brother, and he shakes his head.

"Liam Black was Carmine's most loyal employee. What the fuck is he up to? And what about your team? Are you sure they can be trusted?"

"Their methods may be a little unorthodox, but they come highly recommended, and the guy who recommended them knows the stakes. He won't cross me." His blue eyes brighten as he speaks, and a hint of humor plays across his face.

"Do I want to know this person's name?" I'm arching a questioning brow when he holds up his hand.

"No." The finality in that word, delivered with calculated precision, makes my skin prickle. There are definitely some things about my twin that I am better off not knowing.

We order lunch in since we don't want to miss the package containing the transcript of the call between Danny and Liam. I'm still puzzled by Liam's involvement in this mess. I don't know much about him, but according to Jackson, Black has worked for the family for over two decades and would take a bullet for any of the family members. It sounds like he's turned into a mercenary now. Hopefully, he revealed vital details about what's supposed to happen tomorrow night.

Forty-five minutes later, we're sitting in Courtland's office when a middle-aged man, who I assume is Stan, walks in. He's carrying a small device and places it on the desk in front of us. He moves with ease, as if he's an old friend instead of an employee. "Is there anything else, Boss?"

"No thank you, Stan. Just head back to the location and I'll be in touch later." With that the man turns, giving me a slight nod, and leaves the office.

Anticipation is making me antsy. I get up and pace the room like a wild animal while Courtland connects several cables from the box to his computer. As soon as he says, "Got it," I slide back into my chair.

The computer powers up and a man's voice can be heard. Although the audio is grainy, it's the voice of Liam Black. "Relax, everything's going according to plan. She thinks I'm her ally, her protector, but she couldn't be more wrong."

"What the fuck?" I'm trying to focus on his words in the context of the conversation. Having already heard Danny's side of the discussion, my ears are trained on what Liam's saying. "When will it be done?" I search my brain for clues that will lead us to the end game. We thought we were able to decipher some information based on Danny's words, but now that we're hearing both sides, it isn't quite as obvious. After a few more words, the recording cuts out. That didn't give us much more information than we'd initially overheard.

A storm is brewing on the horizon and my girl has no idea. Evidently she sacrificed herself to save my life, and I suspect that's also why she is rejecting my calls. I get it. There's nothing I wouldn't do for her and apparently the feeling is mutual.

From what we can determine, she is in danger and I need to warn her. With Danny highjacking her calls, I'm not certain how I'll make contact short of bringing in a SWAT team and storming the mansion.

I'm practically climbing the walls with worry when my phone rings. Pulling it out of my pocket, I see my mother's name and my heart drops. Since my dad's latest diagnosis, every time one of them calls, my mind anticipates the worst. "Mom, what's up?" I try to dial my anxiety down a notch when I answer.

"Ben, hello darling. I just got off the phone with Knight and he said you were still in New York." Her bright voice suddenly brings sunshine to this cloudy day. Relief washes over me, but I still don't understand her call.

"Yeah, Mom. Something came up and I'll be here a little longer." I hope she doesn't ask about Julia. I'm not ready to have that conversation yet. "Is everything alright?" There's a pause before she speaks again. "Oh, yes. I was just checking to see if you were okay. I know you were anxious about getting back and auditioning that new band for the hotel." Shit, I forgot about that.

"Uh, yeah about that. I'm going to either reschedule or let Knight take that one." Instead of making excuses, I sigh into the phone and decide to tell her what's going on. Well, maybe not full disclosure, but I'll give her a summary of what's keeping me in the city.

"Mom, everything's going to be alright, but some problems have come up with Julia's family and I don't feel comfortable leaving her." It isn't technically a lie, but I can't tell her Julia's psychotic brother has somehow convinced her to take over one of the most ruthless crime families on the East Coast. Mom has enough on her plate with my dad. No need to bring unnecessary grief to their door. I can sense the atmosphere of our conversation shift before she responds.

"Oh, dear me, Ben. Yes, you stay with her, I'm sure she needs you." I groan under my breath, wanting to end this call quickly. So far, we've managed to keep my parents in the dark regarding all things mob related. As far as they know, Julia and her family simply have irreconcilable differences. I snort to myself. That's the least of my worries. "I'm sorry to worry you. I'll get with Knight and have him take care of things for the audition. I'll be back in Stone Creek by the end of the week, and I'll check on you and Dad then."

We say our goodbyes and a weight lifts off my shoulders. I don't like keeping things from my parents, but this would definitely be too much for them to handle. Maybe I don't give them enough credit, but I would never forgive myself if either of them got hurt because of this circus.

After I call Knight and he agrees to oversee things until I return, including the audition, I turn to Courtland, who has been staring at me through both conversations. His expression betrays nothing, but his body language shows he's on edge. His mouth is set in a hard line, and his arms are folded across his chest as his gaze lingers on my face.

"What are you looking at? You're creeping me out." Although my words sound humorous, there is nothing funny about this situation. I'm about to go off on him when he quirks a brow and stands up grabbing his jacket and heading for the door.

When he reaches the threshold, he looks over his shoulder and gives me a one-shoulder shrug while asking, "Are you going to just sit there, or are you coming with me?" His question takes me by surprise. One minute he's eyeing me like a twenty-four ounce T-bone, and the next he's up and out the door. "Where are we going?" I'm speaking as I move toward him, trying hard to keep up the pace. He speaks matter-of-factly.

"To get your girl."

Chapter
TWENTY
SIX

Julia

It feels like it's been weeks since I left that note for Ben. The days blur into night, I find it hard to eat and I'm not sleeping. The two or three hours I manage a night are due to the mild sedative the doctor ordered. It's the only time I'm able to forget. Most nights I fall into a dreamless sleep, for which I'm grateful. It's bad enough the nightmares follow me through the day without invading my nights.

My heart is shattered and there's nothing I can do to reconstruct it from the shards left in the wake of my self-destruction. The ache is visceral, a physical malady that crushes my very soul.

I've barely left my room, much less the expanse of lush green meadows surrounding the compound. Molly and Tess have called multiple times and Lucy has texted, but I can't bring myself to answer. Somehow, it seems that if I don't talk about it, then it didn't happen.

I'm sitting on the deck sipping some sweet concoction the cook made me. I didn't want to offend her, so I took it and I've been nursing it for almost an hour. The melted ice makes it taste more like melted ice cream than the chocolate mocha whatever-its-supposed-to-be.

It's a beautiful fall day. The gladiolas and chrysanthemums are in full bloom and a hint of honeysuckle wafts through the air, but there's also a chill in the air that has nothing to do with the temperature. They say time heals all wounds, but all the time in the world can't put the shattered pieces of my soul back together again. I just have to remind myself how high the stakes are, and that Ben's life is worth more than my happiness.

I'm staring at the dozen or so missed calls and texts when a new notification pops up. This one is from Tess. A smile touches my lips as I read her words.

> Tess: Julia, hey. I'm worried about you. Ben sort of gave us the lowlights, but I need to hear from you. Please call me or at least text back, so I know you're okay. I need proof of life.

I thought my heart was gone, demolished along with my future, but the pain in my chest suggests otherwise. I hate myself for putting my friends through this, but there's no other way. Maybe one day we can reconnect, but for the foreseeable future, it's best if I distance myself from all parts of my old life.

There is, however, one call I can't put off any longer and when I press the call button she answers immediately.

"Hello." She sounds distracted, like I've caught her in the middle of something.

"Hey Mom." My voice cracks and I pray she can't hear how broken I am. I hear a sharp intake of air before her voice echoes over the line.

"Oh my God, Julia. What are you doing? Ben said you were at the mansion." Her words fly out in one rushed breath. I'm thankful that I don't have to explain. She knows if I'm at the mansion, I've given up. Being here means only one thing. I belong to the Baldonis now. I can't speak. My vocal cords are paralyzed, and my breaths are coming out in shallow spurts. She doesn't need me to spin some kind of lie to satisfy everyone's curiosity, though, because she already knows.

"Julia, Ben told me about your letter." The tears I had been holding at bay are now slowly sliding down my cheeks, hot and shameful.

"Sweetheart, tell me it isn't true. You don't need to worry about Michael anymore. Trust me, he will never come back into your life. I made sure of that. We had a plan, remember? You need to talk to Ben." This time I cut her off, tired of her cryptic messages. I exhale a heavy breath and steel my voice, trying to remove emotion from the situation.

"Mother, I know what Ben thinks, but he's wrong. And I don't trust Danny not to pull some shady shit. Until we can sort this out it's the only solution. I can't have Ben with a target on his back. I won't. Please, I need you to back me on this."

I've never asked for much from my mother and I hope she knows that. Even when she helped me escape Michael's evil clutches, I hadn't asked for her help. But I need her on my side now. After a moment of silence, she finally replies. "Okay, Honey, but please don't do anything that can't be undone. Ben loves you and I know you love him. Trust that love to prevail and please watch your back while you're under that roof."

Tears stain my cheeks. I need to end this call before I lose all composure, and she calls me out for the fraud I've become. After the call, I fall back onto the deck chair and bury my face in my hands.

I've finally cried my eyes dry and my head is aching like the worst hangover ever. I move inside and catch my reflection in the mirror. A small gasp escapes my mouth when I take in the dark circles below my eyes. My face is blotchy from the river of tears I've spilled, and I appear thinner than normal, which is ridiculous since I've only been here a couple of days.

It's early afternoon and I need to make a few business calls, so I wash my face and pull my wayward hair back into a low ponytail before making my way down the stairs.

The office is dark when I enter, but as soon as I breach the door, interior lights illuminate the space. Funny, I'd never noticed that before. Walking behind the desk, I pull out the swivel chair and settle in. The room is imposing. I remember visiting this office when it belonged to my father. The memories it holds aren't necessarily bad, although the bad memories are the most vivid.

Running my hands along the smooth mahogany surface, my eyes settle on the deep scratch embedded in the wooden surface. The obscenity Brando carved with his pocketknife and blamed on me. Of course, our father believed him and took the cost out of my allowance, even though he never repaired it.

I'm sitting lost in my memories when I'm startled by a sudden sound. I yelp and clutch my chest before I realize it's the desk phone. Taking a second to calm my breathing, I clear my throat and pick up the receiver.

"Julia Bernard…Uh, Baldoni." It makes me physically ill to use that name, but if I don't start embracing my new normal now, it will remain foreign.

"Ms Baldoni, this is Harry Thomas, Mr. Carmine Baldoni's financial advisor." I raise an eyebrow at that. Why would my father's financial advisor be calling me?

"Will you hold a moment, Mr. Thomas?" I press the intercom and wait for my new bodyguard, Liam, to enter. Since I'm learning to navigate my new circumstances, I feel like I need him to witness this conversation. After a few seconds the door opens and he strolls in. I motion for him to sit as I place the call on speaker and stumble to come up with something clever to say, but when I open my mouth, eloquence is the last thing I hear in my voice.

"I'm sorry, Mr. Thomas, but I'm confused. How can I help you?" There's a long pause before he speaks again.

"Yes, well, that's why I'm calling. Your father left explicit instructions that upon his passing the elder son would retain my services." I don't know where this conversation is going and I sure as fuck hope he knows of Brando's demise. Not that I'd mind giving him that information.

I'm standing by the window looking out at the courtyard, my mind wandering to a dimpled smile and wicked mouth when I realize I've lost track of the conversation. I'm trying to understand what he just said. I make out the words *check, five million,* and *cash withdrawal* before my mind snaps back to the voice coming through the speaker. My eyes dart to Liam, whose mask of stone is firmly in place.

"I'm sorry. Could you repeat what you just said? There was a break in the connection." I lie.

He huffs in exasperation, clears his throat and I don't miss the low growl he makes. "I said Mr. Baldoni requisitioned a sizable cash withdrawal and I'd like to know if you would authorize the amount?"

I feel as if the wind has been knocked out of me and I wobble on my feet as I scurry over to the chair facing the desk. I don't know what to say. If Mr. Thomas is just calling now, it couldn't have been my father or Brando making the request, but it must have something to do with the Kings. "Who would need that kind of capital?" My curiosity makes it hard to stay quiet. Another pause. Another throat clears.

"Uh, Ms. Baldoni, it was Mr. Daniel Baldoni who made the request." Now *that* I didn't see coming. My mouth falls open and my eyes cut to see that the devil himself has entered the room, looking all smug and unbothered by the baffled expression I must surely be wearing. Liam quickly rises. "I'll check in with the men. Let me know if you need anything, Ms. Baldoni."

As soon as he shuts the door, I pick up the phone and take it off speaker. "Mr. Thomas, I will get back to you on this." After hanging up, I yell, "What the actual fuck Danny? What are you planning to do with five million dollars?" I had definitely found my voice and I fully intended to use it.

His lips form another evil smile that makes my skin crawl. Whatever purpose he has for that much capital can't be good. As corrupt as my family is, they'd never callously throw around that kind of money without a damn good reason.

I'm facing the son of a bitch, my arms crossed in a power move, daggers shooting from my eyes and he still doesn't speak.

"Answer my question, brother, because it seems you need my authorization before the request can be fulfilled." He matches my stare, his face a mask of stone. Finally, he releases a deep exhale and breaks the silence.

"It's just business, Julia Bear. Nothing for you to worry your pretty little head about."

By this point, I'm seething with anger. "Stop calling me that, you motherfucker. And since I'm currently leading this family, whatever business this involves, is my business. So, spill it little brother."

He actually snorts as if this is a game to him and doesn't include life and death choices, which just adds fuel to my fire. I am determined not to lose it completely, but I also can't show all my cards just yet, so I'm walking a fine line here.

Scraping a hand through his dark hair, he levels his lethal gaze at me. For a brief moment, fear strikes my heart, but it's quickly replaced by disgust.

When he speaks again, his voice is lower, as if he doesn't want anyone to overhear us. "Look, Julia, before Brando was killed, there was a security deal in the works. Obviously, it was put on hold after his death. Now that things have settled down and you've come on board, it's time to get back to business." As much as I hate to admit it, he is right.

"But why so much?" I don't know much about security, but that sounds like an exorbitant amount of money. Saving the Baldoni fortune isn't the issue here. Carmine and his father had enough investments, and shady business deals, that we could give away this amount of money every day for the rest of our lives and not go broke. But still, if I am going to take over, I want to be prudent about our spending.

"You get what you pay for Big Sis. We've already lost one sibling to violence. We can't go cheap when it comes to our safety." Yeah, if Brando hadn't taken Lucy and I, he might still be breathing, but I don't mention that. Instead I just nod in agreement.

"If you really think it's necessary." I'll stay quiet on this until I can find out more.

"I do. Oh, and by the way, there's that charity auction that's going on at the Met this weekend. I think you should speak on behalf of the family, of course. It was our father's charity after all."

I almost swallow my tongue at that declaration. I know our family supports many causes, but this weekend's event is supporting efforts to stop sexual abuse of young women. How ironic, but I stay quiet on that one, too.

TONIGHT IS A special night with CEOs and other dignitaries present. I chose a daring black number with a plunging neckline and a slit that crawls up my thigh. If only Ben could see me tonight. My heart sinks as I block his image from my mind. This isn't the time to ponder the what ifs. There is business to attend to.

My plan is to make a statement personally as well as professionally. I've been talking the talk for several days. Now it's time to walk the walk. This event will be the first I've attended as the head of the family and I'm determined to exhibit authority to everyone in attendance.

My hair falls in loose waves over my shoulders and I wear a simple strand of cultured pearls to complement the teardrop ones in my ears. Finally I slip on the ridiculous spike-heeled Louboutins and stumble down the stairs.

Danny suggested we all ride together and for once, I don't object. It would look suspicious if I insisted on taking a separate car, so the four of us pile into the stretch limo and tolerate one another for the ride to the Met. My brothers and sister are well on their way to intoxicated bliss as they raid the mini-bar while we are chauffeured along the streets of Broadway.

A low growl falls from my mouth as I watch them take several shots and my stomach churns. I send a disgusted look toward Danny. "Is this how you intend to show up tonight, totally slammed?" I will play nice in public, but when it is just us, I let my brother know in no uncertain terms exactly how I feel about him.

"Chill out, Julia. Don't be such a buzz kill. We're just trying to relax a bit." I want to slap the smirk right off his face, but I won't stoop to his level, not tonight. Instead, I give him my back and watch out the window as we pass by the lights and sounds of the night. After a few more blocks, we roll to a stop in front of the granite steps of the Metropolitan Museum of Art. As many times as I've visited this iconic museum, the wonder never gets old. The foyer is bustling with people of all ages and social status.

The gala is held in the Alexandria Ballroom, where waiters are busy passing around trays of canapés and champagne flutes. As I step inside the massive space, my eyes land on a small orchestra at the front of the room to the right of the stage. The baby grand piano sits untouched and my fingers itch to stroke the keys. Round tables are adorned with white cloths and crystal candelabras surrounded by greenery. The candelabras and twinkling fairy lights around the room provide the only light for the event.

I take a glass of champagne from a passing waiter and make my way to the table in the front that is reserved for the family. There are six chairs circling the table—two others must be joining us tonight. Just as I reach the table a pair of hands appear and pull my chair back.

Looking up, I don't recognize the man but he's staring at me, as if he is waiting for me to speak. Before I find my voice, he relents. "Good evening Ms. Baldoni. My name is Anthony. It seems I've been assigned to your table." He flashes a million-dollar smile and while he is quite handsome, there is no fire, not even a spark, between us. It's not surprising as my heart belongs to someone else.

He takes the seat to my left. Danny and Joey sit across from us and Angie is at my right side. I'm boxed in. I smile back politely. I do know proper etiquette. I was raised by a Baldoni, after all. At least part time.

Thankfully, the song the orchestra has been playing sounds louder from our seats and I silently thank God that I don't have to make small talk just yet.

When the music stops, an awkward silence fills the air. Muted conversations are playing out around us. When soft notes ring out from the piano, Anthony turns toward me, and something dark passes over his eyes before he clears his throat. "Would you do me the honor of a dance?" Taken by surprise, I blink unceremoniously as he stands and extends his hand.

I sit staring at his hand before I'm brought back to the moment. I give him a tight smile that doesn't quite reach my eyes. "Of course." I place my hand in his and the warmth brings a calmness to my senses. He leads me to the dance floor, but when he places a hand to the small of my back it takes everything in me not to flinch at the intimate gesture. I haven't been touched this way by anyone other than Ben in almost two years. Sucking in a breath, I exhale and will my body to relax. Right now, I'm wound so tight I can barely breathe.

We don't speak as our bodies sway to the music, but I can't shake the nagging feeling that I'm somehow cheating on Ben. Cut it out, Julia. This is your normal now, so you better get used to it. Tears prickle the corners of my eyes and I hide my head in my dance partner's chest to keep him from noticing. With every breath I take, every beat of my heart, I'm thinking of Ben. It's too much. I'm about to rush back to my seat when the music mercifully stops.

Instead of returning to the table, I make my excuses and head for the ladies room. When I'm safely behind the closed door, I let out a breath and make my way to the sink. A stranger is looking back at me from the mirror. A broken shell of a woman who isn't tough enough to hold on to her forever. A woman who allowed fear to rule her heart and in doing so has sentenced herself to a lifetime of loneliness and heartache.

After tucking a wayward strand of hair behind my ear and taking one last lingering look at myself, I walk back out just as Danny is headed to the podium.

What is he doing? It isn't time for my speech, but then, I never asked him for a schedule for this evening. Perhaps he's going to say a few words and welcome our guests tonight. I'm practically holding my breath as he walks to the front. Knowing my brother, anything could come out of his mouth.

I mutter a groan under my breath, but apparently Angie hears me because she reaches for my hand, squeezing it gently. When our eyes meet, she gives a subtle head shake. "Don't worry, he won't make an ass of himself. It's too early for that." My sister is clearly on the verge of an alcohol-induced haze. Under normal circumstances she would never be so chatty. But regardless of her state of sobriety, she isn't wrong.

I release a deep breath, grabbing another glass of champagne from a passing waiter and relax into my seat. I'm able to tune out most of his words, but my ears perk up at the mention of my name. I focus my attention to the podium where Danny stands, and the audience hangs on his every word. He talks a good talk and has everyone fooled by the charismatic charade he has created.

"My sister, Julia, will be speaking later tonight." That's all I catch when applause rings out across the room. Feeling my cheeks pink, I look at the man beside me. He's engaged in a conversation with a woman on his other side, so I take this as an opportunity to slip outside for a little fresh air.

According to Angie, the keynote speaker, which evidently is me, won't take the podium until much later. I don't need long, just a few minutes to clear my head. Hopefully, I'll be back before anyone notices my absence.

I make my way past several tables, stopping occasionally as guests greet me and offer congratulations for my new position, which is absurd. I mean, who gets accolades for being a crime boss? Oh my God! Is that what I am? My steps grow faster until I make it to the door.

By the time I reach the exit, my palms are sweaty and my head throbs. I walk through the doors and lean against the railing as I try to get control of my breathing. After a few minutes, I stand, arms folded across my chest to ward off the cold, and look up into the night sky. Somehow, despite the city lights, I can faintly make out the constellations above. The moon is a saucer above and millions of tiny white lights dot the sky.

I stand mesmerized by the majestic noir, totally oblivious to the sounds around me until I glance at my phone and see several notifications. I have three missed calls and four texts from Ben. My heart rate increases as I pull up the texts and see they're all basically the same.

I'm lost in my thoughts when a voice calls out from the entrance. "Julia, what the hell? Danny's looking for you. It's time." How long have I been gone? My eyes land on my sister, whose dark expression makes my chest tighten and my skin prickle. Panic rings in her voice, which means our brother is on the warpath and everyone better get out of the way.

"Okay, Angie. I'll be there in a minute." I'm not going to cower in fear. He can wait until I'm ready whether that is convenient for him or not. I don't give two fucks. I hear her scoff and move toward the door. I turn and follow her back into the building, wiping my palms on the silky fabric of my dress.

A sense of impending doom settles over me as I put one foot in front of the other, each step weighing me down like an anchor. I'm about to give away another piece of myself and the thing I fear most is that my soul won't be far behind.

Chapter

TWENTY SEVEN

Ben

"How fast can you get back to my office?" I hear the urgency in my brother's voice as he speaks.

"Considering I'm in the lobby now, I'd say as fast as the elevator will take me." He has my attention now. Whatever is going on, it is clear that Courtland doesn't like it.

"Thank fuck." Then the call cuts out. Did the fucker just hang up on me? I don't have long to ponder that question when the elevator doors slide open to reveal my twin. His haggard appearance takes me aback.

"Fuck, what happened to you?" He doesn't answer, just turns and leads me to his office. When I enter, I hear a voice I've become very familiar with over the last few days.

Courtland moves behind his desk while I take a chair across from him. He has the voice recording playing over his computer speakers. This must be the one Stan was talking about, the delayed recording from last night. We sit in stunned silence as Danny and Liam converse, unknowingly cluing us in with their every word.

"We need to tie up a few loose ends." That would be Liam.

Danny replies, "Yeah, no one expected her to be a major player."

"That could be a problem, since you know the venue will be packed. We can't afford collateral damage. There are too many power players to risk it." What is Liam talking about? Tomorrow night, venue, packed? I'm considering his words when we hear Danny's sleazy voice again.

"Don't worry, it's been handled. She's the keynote speaker and when she takes the stage, it will be lights out for sister dear." His devious laugh fills the air and my fists clench as I frantically try to recall where she might be. If I could get to that smug son of a bitch, I'd tear him apart with my bare hands.

While I'm practically crawling out of my skin with frustration, Courtland is furiously typing into his phone. He frowns and begins his search again. After a few muttered curses, he slams his phone on the desk and stalks over to the window.

I'm distracted by his actions, but I don't miss Liam's next words as he laughs. "I can't believe she sacrificed herself for Ben King. I'm just biding my time, waiting for the perfect moment to avenge Michael. I know she's responsible for his disappearance and I intend to make her pay." My sharp intake of breath is followed by a string of curses from Courtland. I'm paralyzed and all color drains from my face. My heart stutters in my chest as I try to dissect what he just said.

"Yeah, she's such a stupid little cunt. She thought by agreeing to lead, we'd have no choice but to spare him. She even went so far as to dredge up one of my past indiscretions as insurance to protect him.

But, when she's out of the way, we'll make an example of the rest of the Kings."

I'm seething by the time the recording comes to an end. Looking at my brother, he has murder in his eyes, and I feel the same way. "We need to find out where they are. If this recording was from last night, that means whatever is happening and wherever she is, it's happening now."

Courtland moves behind his desk and is once again pounding out a message to someone while I'm pacing the room. He's staring at the screen when I look back in his direction. "Got it." Relief floods my mind, but it's short lived when I realize we're operating on old information.

"Where are they?" I manage to keep my voice even. There's no need to panic prematurely but I'm suddenly hit by the memory of her being kidnapped and terrorized by her brother's goons earlier this year. We were damn lucky to get her and Lucy back safely, but we're dealing with a different beast. From the little Julia has told me, Danny is a loose cannon whose ruthlessness far exceeds that of Brando or their father.

"They're at the Met."

By the time we leave the parking garage, traffic has slowed to a crawl.

"Dammit!" I can't help the barely leashed anger rolling through me as cars stop, blocking us in on all sides. We don't have much choice as the Met is twenty blocks from where we're currently trapped in gridlock.

We inch forward block by agonizing block until we're six blocks away and once again we grind to a stop. My frustration builds to a dangerous level as I jerk my seat belt off and bolt from the vehicle.

As I make my way through the streets, I see the Met in the distance and the fear that grips my soul becomes bone crushing. God, I can't be too late. Thankfully Courtland's team was able to infiltrate the Baldoni compound and get intel on tonight's events.

When I reach the steps of the imposing building, I bend and catch my breath before continuing on. Barreling through the door, a man in uniform, apparently security, stops me and asks for my ticket. Fuck that, I don't have a ticket.

That's when I hear applause and catch a glimpse of her through the open door. She's walking to a podium at the front of the room. My heart constricts. She's here and she's alive. I just need to keep her that way.

The security officer is eye to eye with me now, and the scowl on his face lets me know he doesn't plan on backing down. "I'm sorry, sir, but I can't allow you to enter without a ticket." Holding up my hands, I make another attempt to get to her.

"Look, I don't have a ticket, but if you'll let me speak to Ms. Bernard, uh, Baldoni, she'll clear everything up." I can hear her voice clearly now. She's in a vulnerable position, and I can't get to her.

Agitation is short-circuiting my thought processes. Then I see movement behind the officer, Courtland rushes into the building, and he hands the officer a piece of paper.

"Of course, Mr. King, this way, please." I should have known Courtland could get us in. We make our way quickly through the dimly lit room. I glimpse Liam Black standing in the back, talking into an earpiece. My gaze sweeps past him and I'm searching for the one person I need to find. I'm a few tables from the front when she locks eyes with me. Shock turns to disbelief as she stops talking, looks down at her notes, and looks up again, this time not breaking eye contact.

I'm stalking toward her as hushed murmurs echo around me. Mere feet from the stage, I notice the unmistakable red dot when it appears on her chest. She gasps as I reach for her milliseconds before a shot rings out.

Chapter
TWENTY
EIGHT

Julia

The noise around me is deafening as I scramble to make sense of it. All I know is one minute I'm talking about the statistics regarding women in the world who have survived sexual abuse at the hands of their loved ones and the next, I'm being tackled to the floor by rough hands and strong arms.

My breath was knocked out of me when I hit the floor and I'm struggling to catch it. When I feel wetness on my forehead, I manage to get a hand free, touch my head, and see red tinged fingers when I pull it back.

"Are you okay? My God, Julia." Disbelief clouds my mind and suddenly the floor feels like it is falling away from me. My words are a struggle, but I am able to squeak out a weak response.

Utter pandemonium has broken out and although I'm still disoriented, I hear Ben yell at someone. "He's getting away. Find him." His voice is loud in my ear and my head feels like a hard rock band has taken up residence inside my brain.

His touch softens as he pulls me to my feet. Shouts come from all around. When I open my eyes, there are people rushing to the door, tables are upturned, and some people are cowered behind them. Security rushes all around and as Ben gently pushes me into a chair, the magnitude of what happened floods my mind.

My eyes search the room for signs of my family, but not surprisingly, they are nowhere in sight. "Ben, what's going on?" I barely manage a whisper.

He leans toward me and places a finger over my lips. "Shh, don't talk Sunshine." He pushes my hair back to get a closer look at my forehead and growls under his breath. His eyes are dark, and as he shakes his head, curses fall from his mouth. He gently kisses my lips before moving back to grab a napkin off the table. With one hand on the back of my head, he uses the other to hold the napkin over my wound and apply light pressure to it as he whispers reassurances in my ear.

I'm starting to relax into his touch when Courtland hurries to where we sit. Ben looks at him as he reaches the table. "It's just a graze. Did you get him?" I'm trying to pay attention to what's being said, but it's difficult when dizziness is making me nauseous. After a few minutes, someone comes over and replaces the cloth napkin with a warm, wet towel. I smile as I hold it to my forehead. Someone has turned on the overhead lights, and I close my eyes against their harshness.

"The shooter? Yea, we got him. The head rat, no, we didn't get him. All three Baldonis are nowhere to be found."

"Fuck all." Ben is furious and I can feel the rage coming off him in waves as he dabs at my head with the wet cloth. He looks at his brother, his expression ominous. "What next, brother?"

Courtland dips his head and gives Ben a sideways glance. "My team has roadblocks set up in a fifteen-block radius. They won't get far. We'll keep the surveillance in place for the time being."

After Courtland leaves to speak with the officers in the back, something catches my eye and my eyes land on someone lying on the floor just feet from where we sit. Ben tries to shield me, but not before I recognize his face.

"Oh God." It's Anthony. I'm suddenly sucker punched and tears stream down my face. He must have stood just as the shooter aimed. By missing me, the shooter hit him, and it is my fault he is dead.

I sob into Ben's neck while he rubs circles over my back. "Oh, God, Ben. I'm so sorry."

"Shh. It's okay, you're safe." I can't agree with that. An innocent person died and until my brothers are stopped, none of us are safe. I cling to Ben's strong body as he wraps me up in his unyielding arms.

The police fire questions at me until Courtland threatens a lawsuit and Ben is about to commit a crime himself. None of us speak on the way back to my apartment. Thankfully my things haven't been moved to the mansion yet.

As we make our way inside, I stop at the sofa and sink into the plush cushions. Courtland plays the recording and as my eyes widen in horror at Danny and Liam's words, I feel Ben's gentle arms slide around me, pulling me closer.

After everything I've done, all the fail safes I've put in place, we are back to square one with my brother. At least, now I know the full scope of his vile plans.

Just as my eyes close, my phone rings, snapping me to attention. Instinctively I clutch my chest, afraid of what's to come. When I see my mother's name, I heave a small sigh of relief, but my fingers won't move. I hold the device out to Ben, who pushes the green button and places the call on speaker.

"Hey, Katherine, it's Ben." It's possible she already knows about the incident, but on the chance she doesn't, I know he wouldn't want to alarm her, so he keeps his voice casual.

"Ben, where's Julia?" Yep, she knows. The panic in her voice tells me she heard what happened.

"She's fine. She's just resting a bit. The bullet grazed her head, but she'll be alright." I can't believe how calm he sounds. I want to fucking kill someone.

A sharp intake of air comes through the phone. "Oh, thank God. Well, obviously, I needed to check on my daughter, but there's another reason I called." My heart skips a beat as I look at Ben and he shrugs. I can't remain quiet. "Okay, what is the reason for this call?" I don't want to sound rude, but I was almost killed tonight. What can she possibly have to say that even comes close to that? There's a long pause and I'm about to ask if she's still on the line when she speaks again.

"I just got off the phone with my grandfather." My eyes widen again at this statement. I thought he was dead. I'm shaking my head, my eyes glistening with unshed tears.

"I'm sorry, I'm not following you. Did you say your grandfather?" Another pause, and this time it's Ben who breaks the silence.

"Katherine, what are you talking about? I thought your family were all deceased." This is getting more fucked up by the minute.

"My parents are dead, yes, but my grandfather, Edward Tagliaferro is very much alive and living in upstate New York." I'm trying really hard to wrap my brain around what she's telling me, but suddenly it feels like my whole life has been one big joke and I'm the only one who didn't get the punchline. Before I can get another word in, she continues.

"That's a story for another time darling, but you need to hear what I'm saying now. My grandfather, your great grandfather, has powerful connections that reach far beyond Baldoni territory."

As intriguing as this story is shaping up to be, I need her to get to the point. "Mom, what does my great grandfather have to do with any of this?" This conversation is getting old fast.

"It seems Danny Baldoni was involved in some under the table deals behind his father's back. He stole millions from the Tagliaferro family. Ever since Carmine's death, Edward has been looking for the perfect opportunity for retaliation and tonight, he found it. It's over, Julia, and I have Michael's death certificate, as well. You're finally free."

"What?" I can barely hear myself speak. It's over?

"Yes, darling. When my grandfather found out about the hit on you he decided to cut those ties once and for all. He had his own hit precisely orchestrated to take out Danny and tonight, that hit was executed. Danny, or what's left of him is in a smoldering car just outside the city."

Without another word, Ben moves to turn on the TV, and a video of dark smoke fills the screen. "Mom, I'll talk to you later." That is all I manage to say as realization dawns on me. The threat is eliminated. Collapsing back into Ben's arms, I barely register Courtland closing the door on his way out. Ben and I are alone for the first time in days. Joey and Angie can be handled. Maria can be handled. The nightmare is finally over.

We sit in silence, my head resting on Ben's chest, our breathing in sync until he moves me to the side and stands up. I close my eyes, and when I open them again, he is in front of me, down on one knee, holding a small square box in his hands. My breath hitches as I look into his honey gold eyes that glisten with moisture.

He lifts the lid back to reveal an emerald cut diamond surrounded by smaller princess cut stones. I'm suddenly blinking back hot tears as he flashes that King smile that melts my panties and sets my heart on fire. That sinful dimple that I want to lick is on full display and his expression is playful, then quickly turns salacious. He clears his throat.

"Julia Bernard, love of my life. Will you marry me?" I nod my head as tears course down my face.

"Yes, yes, a million times yes. I'll marry you, Ben King." He stands, picking me up in one swift move and spinning me around until we're both dizzy.

"You've made me the happiest guy in the world. We're finally free."

Yes, my Brutal Prince is right. We are finally free indeed. Now it's time to see where the future takes us. We will never be alone again as long as we have each other.

Epilogue

Ben

SIX MONTHS LATER.

We ended up having that Valentine's Day wedding. It was a quick turnaround, but given I'd almost lost the woman I love twice in less than a year, I wasn't taking anything for granted. By a miracle that none of us questioned, my father was able to attend our wedding. That was two months ago. Tonight, we are holding a belated reception at the Lux with our family and friends in attendance. Well, everyone except Knight. He's in another state playing a gig, but he's due back late tonight.

When my phone buzzes in my pocket, a smile creeps over my face. It seems I have been doing that more and more lately. I press the button and wait for the FaceTime call to connect.

"Speak of the devil." I can't help the smirk on my face.

"Love you too, Brother." Knight's face fills the screen, and I can hear music in the background and female voices, lots of female voices, coming from behind him. It appears they've already boarded the plane for Stone Creek.

It doesn't take long before we are all crowded around my phone, giving our youngest brother shit about missing tonight. "Hey, I had this gig scheduled before you and Julia even tied the knot. I offered to cancel, remember? Don't bust my balls."

I laugh because he's right. He'd wanted to cancel after we set the date, but Julia wouldn't hear of it. That's another of the million things I love about my wife. She's always thinking of others.

After we agree to meet up tomorrow for family dinner, we end the call and I pull Julia into a slow dance. "I've waited all night to dance with my wife." She gives a wicked chuckle and wraps her arms around my neck while we lose ourselves in the music. Looking around, I take in the people here with us.

Tess is talking to Lucy about her upcoming nuptials and Molly is playing her heart out at the piano. Julia could have had her pick of musicians, but when I'd asked, she had looked at me like I'd lost my mind, and she let me know about it. According to her, there is no other musician in the country who rivals Molly on the ivory keys. I disagreed, because my wife is at least as good—but then, I'm partial.

When the song ends, I move toward the group table reserved in the back. Molly moves to join the girls and Julia pulls her in for a hug. "You were fabulous as usual."

Molly's cheeks flush as she slides onto Courtland's lap just as Julia moves to mine. Jack is sitting beside Lucy now, and Tess is by herself. After a few minutes of casual conversation, Julia speaks up.

"Where's Dillon tonight?" Lucy groans, but Tess's eyes light up as she lets us know he is out of town and will return in a couple of days. We're laughing and taking shots when someone's phone rings. I'm looking around as Tess pulls hers out and frowns at the screen before answering.

"Hello. This is her." Everyone's attention is focused on the petite blonde at the end of the table. Her face is pale and she looks as if she's seen a ghost.

"Oh my God. Are you sure it's his?" She's cutting her eyes toward me. The fear in her words makes me look toward my brothers and immediately each of our phones receives a text message. A startled gasp falls from Julia's mouth as she reads over my shoulder. Molly places a hand on Courtland's shoulder.

"What is it? What's wrong?" It's Jackson who answers.

"It's Knight. His plane is missing."

Read Knight and Tess's story in

Troubled Knight, Book Four

The Stone Creek Series.

Learn more at www.TamiMason.com

Acknowledgments

Thank you for reading the third installment in the Stone Creek Series. I hope you loved Ben and Julia as much as I did. The number one rule when writing a book is that it takes a village. Once again, there are many people who helped bring this work to print. I will name a few and hope anyone I may leave out will graciously accept my apologies.

Amanda Shepard and Shepard Originals—thank you for another beautiful cover. As always, you never disappoint.

Rebecca Aksdal—You are a Rockstar for stepping in and giving me my voice back. Thank you!

Janis McAdoo—thank you for creating my gorgeous website and entertaining any last-minute requests (there have been many) without complaining. You are the best!

CJ Corbin—my good writing buddy. Thank you for helping me find my motivation when I was in a bad place and the clock was ticking. You're a forever friend and colleague.

Sara Cunningham: What can I say? Thank you for being my special friend. I can't wait for our next adventure.

Tailored Designs—Thank you for the beautiful formatting you gave my baby.

John—None of these pages would have been written had it not been for my best friend and soulmate. You sacrificed every day to make sure I had everything I needed to be successful in this endeavor. Thank you for being my event table manager and my gopher for all things snacks and drinks. Your love and patience carried me through many trials and disappointments. Whenever I thought about calling it quits, you were there, encouraging me and loving me with all you had. You're my forever.

And finally, to you, the reader—thank you for supporting my efforts. I hope you enjoy escaping reality as much as I did, if only for a little while. If you loved Ben and Julia's story, stay tuned for more from the Kings and Stone Creek as we wrap up this series with Troubled Knight, Knight and Tess's story.

Tami Mason

About the Author

Tami Mason is a contemporary and steamy romance writer with the occasional dark romance thrown in for good measure. She lives in a small East Texas town with her husband of forty-two years and three fur babies. When she isn't writing, you might find her with one of her four grandchildren living the dream. Please follow her on the following platforms.

Learn more at www.TamiMason.com